TITAN'S CRADLE
A Novel of the Sensual Suns

by Frank Sol

Chapter One

"So, what do you see out there?"

Jason Shaw turned his head away from the small porthole to glance briefly towards his companions. "Nothing worth talking about, Damian." Then he turned back towards the porthole and continued peering out into space. The distant stars were bright specks against the blackness. "I think I can see the freighter."

"No way, man. We're still too far away."

Jason didn't bother replying. Damian Bowie was the youngest member of Pouncer Squad, though Jason was the newest addition to it. He tried to relax and enjoy the rather impressive view—though his stomach still felt queasy in the zero-gee conditions. *I should be used to it by now,* he thought. He had been past the queasiness for nearly a week. *Until this morning.* Right after the distress signal came in....

First mission jitters, right? Jason thought to himself. *This is why I signed up for that bonus. Earn some increased pay while touring the solar system...that's what the recruiter offered.* But would reality actually match up to the stirring sales pitch? *So far I haven't seen much outside of the* Reckoning's *corridors.*

Damian made a comment in a low voice and several of the other Pouncers laughed.

Jason frowned—he'd missed the comment but caught the laughter. *This is* not *what the recruiters promised.* Still, he was committed to his contract so he might as well make the best of the situation.

The *Private Reckoning* was a *Mediator*-class escort carrier. The Belt Consortium relied heavily on a fleet of similar carriers to support their anti-piracy patrols. The BCM's *Vindicator* and *Liberator*-class gunships were good for fending off attacks, but carriers could cover a lot more territory.

And there's no shortage of empty space to cover, Jason noted. Just keeping track of registered shipping traffic was hard enough, let alone trying to hunt down bands of pirates who struck without warning and vanished just as quickly. *Even telling pirates apart from legitimate freighters is nearly impossible without actually stopping and boarding their ships.* Not that boarding every ship plying the trade routes was even an option....

"We're lucky we were so close when we heard the distress signal." Damian was saying. He rested his hands on his lap. "We'll be able to catch the pirates in the act this time and recover the freighter."

"That should be worth a few credits as a bonus," Brad Kellar commented from where he was strapped into his own chair.

"You'll do anything for an extra bonus," Terry Sisler joked. "Won't you?"

"I wonder if that's why we got the new corporal."

Jason glanced back at them. *I was hoping no one would complain too much about my arrival. The squad needed a corporal. I was the lucky one assigned.* After nearly three weeks on the patrol, he still wasn't sure if someone already in the Pouncers should have been promoted.

"Just be glad it's not a damned star-liner," Franco Morticelli muttered from where he was sitting. At thirty-seven, he was the oldest member of the squad, and apparently had no greater ambition in life other than to keep signing up for duty with shipboard security teams. Nineteen years of such missions had left their mark on him. He kept his head shaved to further play up his *tough-guy* act. "I hate fighting on liners. Too many damned civilians to get in the way."

"It's just a freighter, Franco."

"So what, Joshua?"

"There won't be a lot of crew onboard to start with." Joshua Warner offered a shrug. "A dozen altogether." He made the statement sound like a question.

Franco muttered something under his breath.

If that speck was the freighter, then we should be already be at battle stations, Jason thought to himself. He was still staring through the porthole. *We're well within weapons range if I can see the ship with my naked it.* No doubt he was only seeing some piece of space junk. *Which Damian figured out before I did.*

Reluctantly, Jason turned away from the porthole. The other five men in the tiny cabin were strapped into their chairs trying to pass the time. "You'd think we could get a feed from the sensors or something," he said. "Something to watch."

Terry Sisler laughed at that. "You are still *so* wet." His smirk was matched by a matching grin on Damian's face, who was sitting across the table from him. They were playing cards—the tabletop was magnetized to hold the metallic cards in place.

Jason frowned, but didn't say anything else.

Joshua Warner took a bite out of a ration bar. "The company wouldn't spend the credits to install a monitor and feed for the likes of us," he said between chews. "We're not important crewmen. We're just grunts."

"Keep us all in the dark, like mushrooms," Franco grumbled from his own chair. He was sitting as far away from the rest of the group as he could manage. "That's the way it is...keep us in the dark and shovel some shit on us every now and then."

Damian was laughing quietly. So was Brad.

"You'll get used to it in time!" Franco snapped. "You'll see. The bright-stars just open the door long enough to snap orders and then they ignore us again."

Jason hid his own smile at the term. *Bright-star* referred to pretty much any ranking officer in the Colonial Guard, and the term was rapidly being adopted by the grunts in the Belt Consortium Militia.

Damian shook his head. "Come on, Franco. It's not like that at all!"

"Isn't it?"

"No way." Damian shook his head. "We've just got different duties to perform. If anything, the ship's crew is jealous of *us*."

"Ha, ha, ha!" Franco slapped his leg with his hand as he roared with laughter.

Jason reached for the bulb of juice he had clipped to his belt and took a sip through the straw. The apple-peach juice was tepid now.

The hatch to the small room hissed open and the squad commander stepped through. Sergeant Ian Foster's magnetic-soled boots clicked against the decking. His hair was cut short and spiked with gel. "At ease."

Jason tried not to smile—no one had stood up when the sergeant had entered.

"I've just been on the bridge talking with Captain Davidson." Ian gave the Pouncers a fierce look, as if trying to determine what mischief they might have gotten up to in his absence. "We're coming up on our target. The freighter is moving slowly and the pirates likely have no idea that we were in a position to respond so quickly. This should be a fairly straightforward mission."

"Point-and-shoot, just the way I like it."

Ian glanced towards Franco, but didn't say anything. He was wearing the same general duty uniform as the rest of his squad. The crimson-coloured coveralls were suitable for pretty much any shipboard activity short of actual combat.

Terry and Damian slapped their right hands together.

"This is still slated as a basic search-and-rescue operation," Ian Foster announced to them. "Just a small crew, if any, onboard this one. They should be all pirates." He was holding a small computer-pad in his hand and he paused to check the screen. "From the initial reports, the regular crew were ejected in life pods immediately after the hijacking, so we're not expecting any civilians to still be around."

"Thank God for that, Sarge," Franco growled.

Jason turned back to the porthole one more time. The freighter—if he was really seeing it in the distance, and not fooling himself with space junk—was a slender central fuselage with half a dozen bulky

cargo pods attached. A good design really, as each of the fifty thousand pound pods could be detached at port for loading or unloading while other pods took their place, thus minimizing the amount of downtime that said freighter was not actually travelling the space lanes. *A few hours layover to swap pods and refuel, and then away goes a fresh cargo to some other port. Gotta love the way the mega-corps always watch the bottom line.*

Ian narrowed his eyes, but he was long since used to his squad's personality quirks. "We'll be ordering them to stand down when we reach weapons' range, but I doubt they'll make it easy."

Jason nodded his head in silent agreement. From reports, most pirates put up a fight against police boarders. *Hopefully we can surprise them.* Pouncer squad only had six men. *How many pirates in the crew?*

"Captain Davidson and I have discussed tactics. The freighter is considered to be a free-fire zone, but try to pick your targets carefully, just in case. We're moving in and securing the target, then we'll see what our next move will be."

"How many pirates are we looking at?" Brad Kellar asked.

"Intell is uncertain. There were only eight crewers onboard the *Cattle Drive* to start with, so there shouldn't be more than a dozen pirates there now. A skeleton crew would be all they'd need to fly the ship to their base."

"Human or alien?"

"From early intell, they were just humans."

A couple of the Pouncers breathed a sigh of relief.

Jason was one of them. *Some of those aliens are real monsters.*

"Any chance on tracking them to their base?"

Ian shook his head. "That's beyond our mandate," he told Joshua. "The Colonial Guard want the privilege of destroying the pirate bases."

"Well shit." Franco spoke for everyone.

"And the Colonials are doing such a good job of it." Joshua pursed his lips as if he wanted to spit. "They haven't blasted a base in months."

"Yeah."

"Are they even still patrolling the Belt?"

"The strategies and mission parameters of the Colonial Guard are not our concern," Ian said over the squad's muttering. "We are part of the security forces maintained by the Belt Consortium. We patrol and intercept. We're neither an army or a navy. Full-scale base assaults and invasions are the duty of the Colonial Guard."

Jason grimaced. By Terran Colonial Union law, the BCM was limited in the size of ships it could operate and the types of weaponry it could issue to its personnel. *The government won't allow us to become a viable threat to the Guard. The Senate would not risk a civil war. We're only allowed enough firepower to battle pirates.*

"We have a clearly defined mandate to follow and we will obey the dictates of the law," Ian continued. "If you want to play with larger warships and more powerful weaponry, then you're in the wrong militia. If you want to enlist in the Guard, feel free. Otherwise, you'll listen to my orders." He paused, but no one said anything else.

"We are going to retake the *Cattle Drive*," Ian said. "We are going to secure the bridge and the navigational database. We are going to take prisoners who can then be questioned about the rest of their pirate band.

"And if we manage to locate their base, then it's very likely that Captain Davidson will decide to throw a small party to celebrate. Of course, we'd then have to invite every Consortium ship in the area to join us there."

The squad cheered.

"Now get down to the armoury and draw your gear and weapons. I want us ready to deploy within the hour."

"We're that close?"

"Yes, Damian. We are that close."

"About freaking time." Franco was the first man out of the door. He ignored his magnetic-soled boots to throw himself into the air and swim his way down the corridor. The rest of the squad followed suit.

Jason grunted softly and pushed himself away from the porthole.

Ian Foster nudged him. "Don't be so grumpy, Corporal," he said. "Just because you're not a morning person..."

"I hate getting up when it's dark outside," Jason replied honestly.

"You're out in space—it's always dark outside."

"I know. Don't remind me." Jason sighed and thought back to earlier that particular morning....

Jason leaned back on his bunk. The loose restraint straps held him in place in the zero gravity—he had grown used to the feeling quickly enough—but he still had other problems. He was a healthy young man in top condition and his body was very much a walking, talking, sex machine. *Three weeks on patrol with no chance for sex*, he thought, feeling his raging hard-on tenting out the front of his boxer shorts, *is really too much. What the hell was I thinking? No bonus pay is worth this shit!* His thoughts were suddenly interrupted by a kick from the bunk below him

"Get your ass out of bed!" a voice shouted from below.

Jason sighed. "Already?"

"Yeah. We gotta get ready for the next shift."

Jason groaned and rolled over. The *Mediator*-class escort carrier's thirty-four member crew hot-bunked—the off-duty crew slept in the same bunks as the on-duty crewers. The three officers had their own private cabins, and the thirty-seven fighter pilots had their own bunks separate from the rest. *Could be worse,* he thought to himself. *If the* Reckoning *was in assault mode, there'd be another two hundred and fifty people crammed onboard.*

Jason's buddy—and superior officer—Ian Foster, was already climbing out of his own bunk, and movement was equally obvious in the upper bunk and the three bunks at arms' length across the aisle.

Pushing and shoving in the narrow aisle soon solved the problem of tenting boxer shorts and the seven soldiers carefully avoided looking at each other as they dressed and headed out to a quick breakfast and a new shift. Jason looked forward to his turn in the shower and a few minutes in the head as it was the only chance for some private space—as small as it was—on the ship.

Twenty minutes later with full stomachs, Ian and Jason wandered out of the mess hall and wandered towards the arms locker with the shift change check list and a chance to chat alone with no one else to listen in. Both men wore the crimson-hued coveralls and magnetic-soled boots favored by the Belt Consortium for its ship crews.

"Remember our last night on shore leave and those two girls in the *Fox and Hounds Bar*?" Ian asked. "I could sure use their services right about now."

"Me too!" exclaimed Jason. *Though I'd rather have had the bartender from that place. He was a total hunk. Those tight pants and shirt hinted at everything while showing nothing. I'd have loved to gotten him home and.* He felt his dick twitch in his coveralls.

Ian was making a note on his clipboard. "I was dreaming about those girls last night," he said. "I thought I was going to bust a blood vessel this morning. My cock was so hard when I woke up. Damn. They should have a jerk-off room on board that we could book for some private time."

Jason smiled at the thought, and at this entire conversation. "I thought in class they told us that we could get private time in the head or in the showers. Shit, by the time you back in and sit on the toilet, the space is so small you cannot move. And, with a time limit on each vibe-shower there is only just enough time to wash. I need a little time to get in the mood."

"So, have you jerked off in bed yet?" asked Ian.

"Naw." Jason shook his head, feeling his cheeks growing hot. "I have trouble with the idea of five other guys in the room watching or listening. I heard Franco doing it across the aisle the other night."

"Me too," Ian chuckled. "He does tend to be rather...energetic. I was afraid he was going to shoot across and hit me in the face."

Jason laughed somewhat sheepishly. He'd been listening to Franco as well. *I bet half the ship can hear him!* "Maybe the captain would rent out his private quarters for ten minutes to each crew man once a week for a good private session. Do you think he would go for that?" Jason said with a slight smile on his lips.

"Now that would be one to boast morale on these long patrols," Ian agreed. "Still, there are other methods."

"Oh?"

"Yeah, we adapt." Ian fell silent as the hatch to the room clanked open. "So after you get done with sweep..."

Jason was impressed at how quickly Ian was able to switch the topic of conversation as other crewmen entered the locker and new work assignments were passed around.

Ian didn't so much as glance at him again.

As Jason left the room and headed out to his shift assignment, he wondered what the rest of the ship's compliment did to relieve the pressure. He was still hard in his coveralls, but he hoped no one would notice. The *Reckoning* was entirely crewed by men—for whatever reason—and it would be in space for at least three more weeks before getting any shore leave on Mars.

Three more weeks before I have a chance to visit a recreation house, he thought in annoyance. *Damn.* He had to find a solution or else he'd burst.

How quiet can I be in my bunk? he wondered. *How fast in the showers?*

· **Chapter Two**

Jason swallowed in a suddenly dry throat as soft hoot of an alarm brought him back to the present and his current problem.

An impending boarding action.

Just like the simulations, he told himself. *Just do what we did in training and everything will be fine.* His boots kept him firmly anchored to the deck, though the rest of his body swayed slightly in the zero-gee.

"I guess it's time to lock and load." Damian Bowie's words were calm, though his voice was anything but.

"Just point and shoot," Franco growled. "And try not to hit me this time."

"It was an accident!" Damian protested, throwing up his hands. "Accident, Franco. Jeez. And it was only that one time."

Franco growled out a curse.

Ian Foster was standing in front of them, with his eyes half-closed. "Captain Davidson has just ordered the *Drive* to stand down and prepare for boarding. No response yet."

Jason swallowed again. *Here it comes.*

"Check your gear," Ian ordered. "Then your buddy's. You all know the drill."

Body armour creaked softly as the assault team checked each other's equipment one more time. The small cabin felt even more cramped than normal, now that they were suited up. The *Coleman MA-4* body armour consisted of a Kevlar-based jacket and pants, to prevent knife damage, with torso plates for added protection against ballistics and PPG bursts.

"Check your weapons."

Jason heard Ian's order and looked around.

Two of Pouncer Squad were armed with rifles—the powerful *Mauser CG-749-AC* Heavy Phased Plasma Guns. The others carried

Edgars CG-TC4 WebCaster rifles, and every man had a *Mauser CG-7* PPG pistol at his hip.

Ian was glaring at him.

Jason hastily checked his WebCaster, but it looked ready for action. *No civilian tech here, for all that the Belt Consortium is little more than corporate security*, he thought. *We're not Colonial Guard but we're still tough.* The various companies which made up the Consortium did not stint on arming their security teams, however closely they came to skirting the law. *Given the way the scheming and plotting goes on, I half expect to see us armed better than the Guard.*

That thought sobered him and he quickly bent his head to check his weapon more closely. *People talk about a brewing civil war, but surely no one would be that stupid. If we show any signs of weakness, one of the alien governments will sweep in and conquer us.* Only by showing strength could Earth and its colonies remain independent.

A soft hiss followed a crackle of static in his helmet. *"Comm check."*

"Working fine, Sarge." Terry Sisler tapped his helmet—every helmet had a built-in comm-link, but sometimes they fizzled out. "We hear you."

Joshua and Damian were standing next to each other, whispering softly.

Jason swallowed. "Almost time then."

Brad gave him a *thumbs up* gesture. He was wearing his usual pre-combat grin. It made him look like an half-deranged idiot.

Jason rolled his eyes.

"We've launched our fighters." Franco had tapped into the *Mediator's* intercom system and was listening with his eyes closed. "They're going after the freighter's engines."

"A good plan...disable it so it can't run."

"A corporate freighter can't outrun a carrier." Damian shook his head. "We've got a lot more speed."

"And a dozen fighters which can fly rings around even the fastest freighter," Joshua added. "I'd put money on a *SkyWolf* over a *Zephyr* any day. Assuming the pirates even have fighter escorts."

Jason knew full well that freighters weren't equipped to carry fighters, though some cargo pods could be modified into impromptu hangers. *Even so, we'd only face seven fighters. And we'd see the pods opening up, so we'd have plenty of time to blast them with our weapons. The freighter would never survive long enough to launch any fighters.* Still, the mission would not be easy…. "The pirates could try to shoot us."

"With their popguns?" Franco laughed loudly. "They'd miss more shots than they'd land." He shook his head. "Don't be such a pansy."

"Look, I'm just saying—"

"The pirates won't want to start a firefight. The *Reckoning's* blast cannon could tear that old freighter into pieces. No, they'll let us get in close and board. The pirates are like me…they like it up close and personal."

"Now there's a mental image I didn't need," Terry joked. "Bad enough we have to listen to you in your bunk at night."

"If you don't like watching me work my magic, then don't watch." Franco gave the other man a grin. "You're getting drool all over your pillow."

Brad's laugh was the loudest.

"Cut the chatter guys. The shuttle is prepped so let's get onboard." Ian smiled behind his visor. He'd already sealed his helmet, even though the risk of combat was still minimal. "Our fighters have convinced the pirates to cut their engines. We're going over." He tapped the side of his helmet. "This is where we earn our bonus pay."

"If I wanted to do this, I'd have joined the Colonial Guard and gone off to fight the Takakas," Jason grumbled sourly. He was a security guard, not a marine. Of course, he had gotten to know a few

Groundpounders during leave sessions...that one sergeant had taught him more than few new *wrestling* moves....

Damian cursed softly as he bent over the small keypad. He had the cover off and had reconnected some of the wires.

Jason took a deep breath, trying to steady his nerves. The air in his self-contained suit was too dry and it smelled metallic.

The small shuttle had left the *Reckoning's* hanger and zipped quickly across the short space between the carrier and the hijacked freighter. Everyone had held his breath during those few minutes. The freighter might only carry four light particle beams, but even those weak weapons would have been more than sufficient to burn through the shuttle's hull and kill the boarding party.

But the worrying was needless and the shuttle landed on the freighter's hull and the pilot managed to synch up their airlocks. The BC *SkyWolves* buzzed the hijacked ship, trying to distract the pirates.

"What's taking so long?" Ian demanded.

"They changed the codes." Damian tried again. "Damn it." The Pouncers had been given the usual access codes from the *Drive's* owners after being assigned to retake the freighter, but those codes were no longer valid. "I can't get the decoder to work either." The small computer-pad in his hand should have been more than capable of breaking through the locking codes and opening the lock. "They must have some good tech."

"We don't have time for this." Ian hefted a S-30 *FlashBang* grenade in one gloved hand. "Franco, you do it."

"Got it." Franco pulled Damian away from the keypad. "Watch how a real man opens a door." He inserted a small device into the pad's interior. "Boom." The thermal charge ignited and melted through the wiring with a loud hiss.

The hatch slid open.

"Now!" Ian exclaimed and two grenades were tossed through the opening.

The explosions from the *FlashBangs* were loud, even with their helmets on.

"Go, go go!" Ian snapped.

The Pouncers leaped through the hatch and into the airlock. They twisted through the air, easy in zero-gee, and managed to get their boots into contact with the deck.

The inner airlock was deserted.

"Wasted grenades." Franco was holding his rifle ready for action and seemed quite disappointed that he had no viable targets. "They should've been waiting for us." He glared at Damian. "We took long enough breaking in."

"Not my fault," Damian replied. He hooked his thumb towards the keypad on the bulkhead. "They've pulled the wires." That was a much better means of preventing entry than simply encrypting the passcodes.

Terry cleared his throat. "Not entirely wasted." The inner airlock door was open and the dimly-lit corridor had three crewmen floating lifelessly in mid-air. The trio were human, wearing ordinary clothing. PPG rifles were floating nearby, having been dropped when the pirates were knocked unconscious.

"The morph gas wasn't wasted." Jason guessed that all three must have gotten a good lungful and now they'd be asleep for hours.

Ian adjusted the manner in which he was holding his WebCaster. "Let's try to reach a ventilation junction and see if we can hack the life support."

Jason hoped so. It would make their job so much easier if the pirates could be neutralized by flooding the air ducts with morph gas. But he wasn't holding his breath.

The squad began to move down the corridor, stepping carefully so that their boots kept them attached to the deck. The pilot sealed the shuttle's airlock behind them, to prevent the pirates from hijacking it.

"I wish they had better lights." Joshua was grumbling as he took point—he always grumbled when he was assigned to point. His body armour creaked softly. "You can't see worth a damn in here."

"Keep moving." Ian kept his voice soft. "Full sweep, by the numbers."

A figure moved in the shadows up ahead.

"Take him!"

Joshua Warner hefted his WebCaster rifle and squeezed the trigger. The rifle coughed sharply and launched a thick glob of webbing down the corridor.

"Gah!" a woman's voice cried out.

"Got one." Joshua hurried forward.

The woman was wearing a grease-stained drab blue coveralls. She was stuck to the bulkhead, wrapped within sticky strands of webbing which were still constricting and hardening. She was struggling, but she couldn't break free.

"She's not going anywhere." Ian nodded his head in appreciation. "Good shooting."

Joshua nodded back.

"That's four down already." Brad moved closer to her. "So how many left?"

"You heard the question." Ian turned back to their immobilized prisoner. "How many other pirates are onboard?"

"Go and fuck yourself, Grunt."

"How many pirates are onboard?" Ian repeated.

She spit at him.

"The Sarge asked you a question." Franco swung his rifle around so that it was pointed directly at the woman. "*I* ain't gonna ask as nicely."

She went pale, staring down the barrel.

"Franco, you shoot her with that and she's gonna fry." Joshua shook his head. "Let me get out of the way first." He moved further up the corridor. "Now you can shoot her."

"One last time," Ian growled. "How many pirates are—"

"Ten us of got flight duty!" she burst out. Her voice was breathy and desperate as she managed to tear her gaze away from the rifle to focus on Ian. "It was supposed to be soft duty. A milk-run."

"Four down, seven to go."

Terry chuckled. "Too easy, man."

A crackling ball of plasma splashed against the bulkhead.

"Cover!" Ian snapped as the woman screamed.

Jason peaked around the corner of the bulkhead. "Shit!" A plasma bolt passed him so close that he could feel the superheated bolt of helium on his cheek. He fired a burst from his WebCaster even though he had no target.

More plasma crackled past them.

"Damn it...I knew there'd be a security team." Ian fired a few rounds from his *Mauser*. "Try to focus on targets."

"How can you see any?" Terry demanded as counterfire splashed against the bulkheads.

The smell of ozone was getting stronger, overwhelming the ship's ventilation system.

"We don't want to get pinned down!" Franco pushed himself forward, diving around the corner and triggering his heavy PPG Rifle. The superheated bolts of helium plasma were the same as what the pistols were firing, only a lot more powerful. Even so, the bolts still dissipated quickly around hard materials to prevent damaging equipment or puncturing hulls.

Someone screamed as a bolt struck its target.

"Go, go, go!" Ian ordered.

Jason threw himself around the corner, twisting through the zero-gee, and he desperately scanned the area for a target. A half-seem shape moved and he sent a burst of webbing hurtling towards it.

Franco was still shooting wildly. His rifle was pumping out coconut-sized balls of plasma which hissed down the corridor and splashed against the bulkheads. He bounced off the ceiling.

Return fire was sporadic—two, maybe three pirates were trying to fight back. Their own plasma shots were pistol-sized bursts.

Brad, Terry, and Damian added their own WebCaster bursts.

"Cease fire!" Ian called out as the enemy fire ceased.

The Pouncers obeyed.

After a few moments, Ian waved them forward.

Joshua and Franco were the first to push ahead, the others following.

Jason swallowed.

One pirate was pinned to the bulkhead by webbing. His face was burned and smoking, and there were more charred patches on his arm, chest, and legs.

"Dead." Terry stepped away, looking grim. "You smoked him, Franco."

"He shot first." Franco sounded completely unapologetic. He was swapping the depleted ammo pack out of his rifle with a fresh one.

"He's just a pirate." That was what Jason had to remind himself. *This is not some bloodless hacker attack stealing some credits. This is piracy. Real-life piracy.* Everything short of broadswords and walking the plank. The sweet smell of burned meat was heavy in the air.

Ian turned his attention away from the other two pirates. They were also webbed to the bulkhead.

Terry checked on them. "Minor burns, but they'll live." He injected them with something from his medical kit. "Sedatives. They'll be in less pain."

Franco muttered something.

"And they won't be able to break free and shoot us in the back," Terry added.

"I could shoot them now and they won't ever feel any pain."

"No, Franco," Ian said in a sharp tone. "We're not murderers."

Franco grimaced.

"Not even for pirates." Ian took a breath. "Get to the bridge. There's still at least three pirates more unaccounted for. Brad, take point."

The corridors of the freighter were deserted as the Pouncers made their way slowly through towards the bridge. Even without encountering resistance, Ian Foster insisted that they check each room as they passed by.

"We don't want to find anyone ambushing us after we've gone by," he explained.

"Damn waste of time." Franco seemed more annoyed by the lack of additional firefights than by the searching. He kept swinging his rifle from side-to-side, as if he expected to be charged at any moment.

The bridge hatch was locked.

Ian tried one of the pass-codes did not look at all surprised when the hatch remained firmly locked. "Override it."

"You got it." Damian popped the cover open and placed a small lock-picking device onto the exposed wiring. It hummed softly.

"This is taking too damned long," Franco muttered as he looked up and down the corridor, his heavy rifle held ready for immediate firing. "Hurry it up, kid."

"I'm doing the best I can."

Ian nodded to his squad. "Prep an S-40."

Terry nodded. "Ready."

The lock picker beeped and Damian smiled. "Got it."

Ian nodded to Franco.

The hatch hissed open.

"Now!"

Terry threw the grenade through the opening and it detonated.

Ian paused a few moments, then waved his team in.

Five pirates were unconscious, pistols and rifles floating near their hands. Two were still strapped to their seats, while the other three were floating in the air.

Ian let his squad secure the room—Brad stood by the hatch, guarding the corridor outside. They all kept their helmets sealed against the morph gas which still hazed the air. "Five of them. She lied to us."

"Yep." Terry was already checking the unconscious pirates.

Damian and Jason began collecting weapons.

"Good thing we didn't have a firefight," Damian commented as he looked around the bridge. "These guys are packing some serious heat."

"Aw, I was looking forward to a little fun." Franco gave one of the pirates a kick. "These clowns couldn't have stopped us."

The apparent captain was slumped over the navigation console.

"Is the navigational database still intact?" Ian demanded. "Did they have a chance to wipe the memory?"

"I'll check." Jason grabbed the back of the man's head and pulled him away from the console, allowing him to float loosely in the air. *Not half-bad,* he thought as he studied the man's square-jawed face. *For a pirate, that is.* He gave himself a shake. *Work, focus on your work.*

Ian had activated his helmet-comm and was updating the *Reckoning* on their successful capture of the bridge. "No casualties on our team," he added. "Eleven pirates still breathing, one dead. Still checking the nav database." He looked towards Jason.

"Uh..." Jason looked at the screens. "I think the database is intact. Damian, can you take a look?" He wasn't a computer tech after all.

The other man hurried over. "Let me see...." He typed in a few commands.

Jason let him play. He decided to rifle through the captain's pockets. They were empty of pretty much anything personal. "No identicard." That would not matter once the company was able to sample his DNA and run it through the government database. *Every single person in the Union is listed in there.* He reached under the man's leather jacket and removed a pistol from its holster. "Hey, nice piece...it's a *Mauser CG-7* PPG."

Ian approached him. The pistol looked just like his own. "Restricted tech...I think the trial just got more interesting."

Jason nodded. Civilians weren't supposed to have *CG-7s* after all. They were restricted to the slightly less capable *Wesson & Grummen Model-10* PPG which had half the shots and a shorter range than the military grade *Mauser*. "Did you expect anything different for pirates?"

"Nope."

Ian was looking around the bridge. "You all did good," he said. "I'll have a full debriefing with each of you later, but overall I'm satisfied."

"You should be," Franco told him. "We kicked their asses."

"And with no casualties," Damian reminded them.

"And no friendly fire," Franco growled back.

Jason shook his head.

· **Chapter Three**

Connor Davidson, the *Reckoning's* captain, was wearing a *FujamiLink* Headset on his head; it looked like a DRS-28B—the latest model. He floated across the freighter's bridge and grabbed at one of the consoles to stop himself. He swung his boots to the deck so that the magnetic soles could connect and hold him in place. "Well, Corporal?" His dark red coveralls fitted him well enough, though it failed to completely mask his potbelly. Ship crewers had gold fabric for the arms and gold stripes on the legs.

"The *Cattle Drive* has been fully secured," Jason replied calmly. *Which was fairly obvious, otherwise you'd not be over here yet.* He was still wearing his body armour, though he had cracked the visor open now that combat was done with. "No other pirates have been found and the cargo appears to be intact. At least from the initial check of the manifest—a full check still needs to be done."

Davidson shook his head. "That can be done when the *Drive* reaches port. We don't have the time or facilities to conduct a full cargo inspection."

"Yes, Captain." Jason had been fairly certain that would be the response, but he wanted to make a full report. *Some captains do like random spot-checks after recovery operations.*

"What about the prisoners? You caught all twelve pirates?"

"Yes, Captain. The living prisoners have been taken to the *Reckoning* for medical treatment and preliminary interrogation." The dead pirate was likely in cold storage in a cargo bay...or already spaced.

"No civilian prisoners?"

"None. The pirates put them all in the life pods when the seized control."

"How merciful of them."

Jason doubted that very much. *They just don't want to face murder charges if they ever got caught. Piracy is usually simple jail time, but murder is a lot more serious.* One of the few crimes punishable by the death penalty.

Connor finished his inspection of the *Drive's* bridge. He looked pleased by how intact it was—some firefights left the recaptured ships in dire need of major repairs. "Did they have a chance to wipe the database?"

"Damian—Private Bowie—doesn't think so," Jason replied. "They managed to lock it though, with some unusual encryption so we're not entirely sure. We're still working on unlocking it."

Connor snorted loud enough that crewmen on the bridge glanced towards him. He glared and they turned back to their duties. The crewmen were all from his ship, after all, temporarily assigned to operate the freighter until a corporation crew could arrive. "The pirates were going somewhere...they must have programmed the navi-comp with the location of their base."

"Yes, but Damian said that their captain tried to wipe the coordinates when we were storming the bridge. He didn't actually wipe them, but the navigation database—"

"Damn." Connor cut him off. "I'll want that database copied immediately. We'll let our own techs examine it." He tapped his link. "Make it a priority," he told whomever he was talking with.

Jason grimaced.

Ian floated across the bridge. He had removed his helmet, and the rest of his body armour, and restyled his short hair. "Prisoners have been secured back aboard ship, Captain. I see that you've assigned a prize crew to fly the ship back to Mars. Do you need me to assign a security team for the voyage?"

"No, there should be no need now." Connor shook his head. "You and your men can return to the *Reckoning* and get some rest."

"Thank you, Captain."

"Anyway, once our techs, or your private," he added in a more condescending tone, "get the database unlocked, you'll need every man you've got."

"True enough," Ian agreed.

"If we can find the pirate base, then it will have to be dealt with. I have been very carefully reading my standing orders. There's a little bit of room for creative interpretation of those orders should we stumble upon a pirate base during a routine patrol."

"And you can alter our patrol course?"

"Random course changes are allowed, to try and surprise pirates expecting us to be elsewhere." A cruel smile had spread across Connor's face. "We need to wipe out these scum. They're getting much too bold and the Colonial Guard aren't doing enough to hunt them down."

Ian nodded. "I know, Captain."

Jason was in silent agreement. He had lost friends a year ago when the Scrap Yard Gang had raided Jasmine Station, near Io. *They've never been caught either.*

"Come on, Jason," Ian tapped him on the shoulder. "Let's catch the shuttle."

"So how did you like your first real action?"

"It wasn't like the simulators," Jason admitted as he walked along the freighter's dimly-lit corridor. The lighting was even dimmer now than during the boarding action. *The crew claim that they're running computer checks and diagnostics, but I think they're just trying to save on energy costs. Damned credit-pinchers.*

Ian was smiling. "It never is. You handled yourself well though."

"I *have* taken part in combat before."

"Yes, but firefights on a planet aren't anything like fighting on a ship."

"No...."

"And PPGs aren't like slugthrowers. Less recoil, less noise, seemingly less real. Almost makes the fight into a video game. A slugthrower is a lot more real though."

"I know that. I've used both weapons in training." The phased plasma guns were a lot more commonly used now, and not just on ships and space stations. He said as much and Ian nodded.

"PPGs are easier to use. Less temperamental in terms of environment. As for their growing prevalence, carrying one type of weapon is easier than trying to keep track of two. Especially for civilians. Everyone knows that a bullet can puncture a bulkhead as easily as a person...and the end result is just as messy."

Hull breach. No greater fear for anyone in space. Jason failed to suppress a shiver. *You never forget that whistling sound of air leaking out.*

They kept walking.

Jason let out a quiet sigh. "It was all over so fast. You got all hyped and eager and then the gunfire starts and then what?"

Ian slapped him on the shoulder. "So now you take a shower and get some chow. Let the combat rush leave you."

Two crewmen moved past them, away from the airlock, muttering about the need for making a skinwalk on the liberated freighter. They were wearing *EnviroCom* spacesuits, though each man was simply carrying his helmet. The suits were compartmentalized so that in the event of a rip or tear, the wearer would not be exposed to the vacuum of space.

"I'm not spending the whole eight hour shift in this thing," one was saying.

"It shouldn't take that long to check the thrusters ports. Just relax."

Jason sighed and tried not to turn his head around and stare. *The one on the left looked cute, but how can you tell in that suit?* He gave himself a shake. It was pretty much time for bed, not that he was tired. *I'm still wired from combat,* he thought. *I need to work off some of this tension.* But he need privacy for that...and privacy was in very short supply back onboard the *Mediator.*

* * *

Jason's eyes remained open, despite the late hour, and his mind quickly recalled where he was—in his bunk onboard a Belt Consortium *Mediator*-class escort carrier. He had worked towards this particular career for years and now he was beginning to wonder if he had made a mistake.

I wanted a chance to see the galaxy, he thought. *Earth is establishing more and more colonies all the time. Ships are carrying explorers and diplomats and merchants to dozens of alien worlds. We're meeting all sorts of new species. This is probably the most exciting era in history.*

And what better way to get out and see the new worlds and meet new races than by serving with the Consortium? *Get to travel on spaceships and not have to pay for anything.*

Even the chances of actually seeing combat were slim. *The Guard are the ones who are going to end up doing any of the real fighting. The BCM just battles the odd pirates.* In theory. Of course, if some hostile alien power decided to try and seize control of the Solar System, then the Belt Consortium Militia would be fighting right beside the Guard.

Jason yawned and finally managed to fall asleep.

Much later in his bunk again, Jason awoke to find his bladder full and issuing an urgent need to get to the head. He made his way there as quickly and quietly as he could, finding it deserted. Afterwards, he slowly made his way back to the sleeping cabin.

There were no sounds from any of the seven bunks in the narrow space other than deep breathing.

Good, he thought in relief. *Everyone is asleep for sure.*

Jason stood mid-bunk and was just about to climb up and slip into his bed when he felt a hand on his ankle. He quickly realised that Ian was awake and had reached out from the bottom bunk and gently grabbed him. Resisting the urge to say something, he just stood there and kept his mouth shut waiting to see what would happen.

Ian's warm hand slowly slid up Jason's leg, stopping when his fingers reached the leg of his cotton boxer shorts.

Jason didn't move a muscle as the hand remained on his leg.

After a pause, Ian's hand continued moving, slipping under the cotton, and his fingers gently touched Jason's balls.

Jason moaned softly. Even that slight contact was enough to give him an instant hard-on. *Damn,* he thought, looking down at it. His erection was protruding from his shorts into his bunk. He reached down and wrapped his own fist around his cock and slowly stroked it. Up and down, up and down. He spread his legs slightly to give Ian's hand more room to move and almost immediately felt his balls being held and caressed.

Jason's stroking quickened and he bent his knees slightly. Ian took the hint and his fingers moved behind his balls and applied pressure between his legs. It took only two more strokes before Jason felt himself shooting loads of cum into his bunk in his first orgasm in weeks. It took all his self control to keep his mouth shut and hold in the groans of pleasure.

Ian sensed what had happened and his arm withdrew into his bunk.

Shit, what I am doing? Jason suddenly realised the risk they had just taken and he quickly slid into his bunk, ignoring the wet spots on the sheets. *I hope it dries before anyone notices.* He adjusted the loose strapping which kept him from floating out of bed. He listened carefully, but there was nothing except slow breathing and snores from the other bunks. Obviously no one was aware of what had just happened.

Good. Lying in his bunk, Jason felt a slight pressure on his back from below. *What the hell?*

Ian prodded him again.

Well, it's only fair, right? Jason rolled over onto his stomach and let his arm fall over the side of his bunk, sliding down a little with his legs raised so that he was reaching downwards at the just right spot in Ian's sleeping space. His aim was almost on target—he felt the head of Ian's own erect cock lying against his flat stomach. Jason slid a little lower in his bunk and wrapped his fist around Ian and began a slow stroke. Ian's response was a slight humping of his hips as if he was fucking Jason's hand.

After a few minutes, Ian pushed Jason's hand lower and began jerking himself off. Jason took the hint and cupped Ian's balls and then reached even lower to apply pressure between his legs. In seconds, Jason heard Ian catch his breath sharply and he knew that Ian had reached the point of no return.

Jason withdrew his arm and quickly fell asleep.

* * *

Morning came and Jason rolled out of his bunk, feeling relaxed for the first time in weeks. For once, he wasn't experiencing a severe case of morning wood.

"Did you sleep well?" Ian asked. He was wearing a dark red coveralls, with the front partially unzipped to show the grey tee-shirt he was wearing underneath. His hair was gelled and spiked.

"Yeah, thanks." Jason felt his face grow hot and he quickly looked around.

The rest of the squad were nowhere in sight.

"You overslept."

"Did I?"

"Yes, but we're still on post-mission duty rosters so no one cares." Ian shrugged. "I bet most of them will be sleeping the day away."

Jason pulled a tee-shirt on and reached for his duty-coveralls.

"A lot of guys have trouble sleeping after their first combat mission."

Jason glanced towards Ian.

The sergeant shrugged. "It affects everyone differently."

"I'll keep that in mind."

"Anyway, that wasn't really very much in terms of actual combat."

"It wasn't?" Jason finished pulling on his boots.

"No, I was actually hoping for a really good firefight."

Jason grimaced. "Better luck next time."

"You get a better bonus if there's combat. A few anti-pirate combat missions and you'd have the credits to retire on. Well," Ian amended with a grin, "at least be able to take a year's vacation."

"You know what the company says about combat." Jason paused. "'If you want combat, go join the Colonial Guard.'"

"Yeah, yeah." Ian shrugged his shoulders. "It doesn't matter to much right now. It looks like we're going to miss out on any more fighting. At least on this voyage."

"Oh? Did the pirates wipe the database?"

"From all appearances, yes they scrambled it before the freighter was retaken." Ian frowned. "At least we've got a chance of some decent R&R time though."

"Why is that?"

"The freighter's cargo pods are full of starship components. Engines and power systems. High priority stuff for the Guards, and very valuable. Extremely important." Ian chuckled.

"I thought those cargos usually travelled in convoys." The factories which produced ship components were usually located close to the actual shipyards, or else sent production supplies to their destinations in well-protected convoys. *The Consortium Militia usually supplies the escorts. A carrier and several gunships, depending on the value of the cargo. Starship components should have rated at least a* Liberator *or two.*

"There was a drive shortage at the Phobos Yards. Sato-Hyundai decided to send a lone freighter in on a priority run, rather than wait for the next scheduled convoy." Ian shrugged. "Apparently the *Drive* was chosen because head office thought no one would think to attack it. The *Drive* is famous for carrying agricultural equipment out to new colonies."

"The gamble failed."

"Yeah."

Jason wondered if the hijacking had been fluke, or if it was the result of a pirate-loyal corporate spy.

"In any event, Captain Davidson has chosen to return to Mars ahead of schedule, as an escort for the freighter."

"So we're going to have some early R&R?"

"Yeah, down on Mars."

Jason shrugged.

"Oh, it's not all that bad of a place down there," Ian told him. "You just need to get away from Dome-One and all the rabid pro-Earthers."

"Spoken like a native."

"Born and bred on Mars." Ian did not sound apologetic or embarrassed. "The Consortium doesn't give the Earther bias much thought."

"So when we will reach Mars?"

"Two days or so." Ian glanced at his watch. "I've got a briefing to attend. Get yourself some breakfast and enjoy the free time."

"I'll do that." Maybe he'd go and spend some time in the gym working out. Keeping muscle tone and mass was a never-ending struggle while in zero-gee missions.

Ian slapped him on the shoulder, then headed down the corridor.

* * *

Jason managed not to jump as he felt Ian brush up against him.

Every time he touches me, I jump. Lately, he was as jumpy as a schoolgirl on a date with her first crush. *I do not have a crush on my superior officer,* he thought. *We just jerked each other off one night in the bunks. Nothing more.* That sounded absurd even to his ears.

None of the others seemed to be aware of the nocturnal encounter. The jokes and intra-squad rivalries continued no differently and Ian remained friendly and did not allude to the encounter.

Maybe he wants to forget about it. Jason could understand that. *We're serving onboard the same ship. Everyone says shipboard romances are doomed to failure...and once they go bad, there's no way to avoid your Ex.*

"Look at them." Ian gestured towards the porthole. "You can see the shipyards."

Jason looked. It really was a sight worth seeing. The immense factories were long cylinders with a retractable door on one end. They did not rotate and were little more than a framework designed to support the construction process. The actual manufacturing of the ship components took place in various companies located throughout the Union, which were then shipped to the closest Yards for actual assembly. "It looks very phallic."

Ian glanced at him. "You have a one-track mind."

"I know." Jason wished he could restart the conversation. "I don't envy the yard dogs." The labourers worked in zero-gravity conditions—it would be quite impossible to assemble even the smallest space-going vessel on the ground—completely reliant on double-reinforced spacesuits for protection. "Not an easy job."

"No, but they get paid well enough."

The small cabin remained empty and both men kept looking out of the porthole.

"So have you enjoyed your first patrol?"

"Yeah, I guess I have." Jason nodded. "It makes a change from serving on one of the transfer stations or down on a moon."

"That it does." Ian chuckled softly. "You looking forward to getting back into some gravity?"

"Yeah, isn't everyone?"

"Pretty much. I know this little place down in Quebecneuve." Ian smiled widely as he said that. He reached down and gently rubbed his crotch through his coveralls. "Caters to a very select clientele."

"Down there?" Jason licked his lips. He could see Ian's hard-on clearly outlined against the crimson fabric of the coveralls.

"Where'd you plan on going for your vacation time? New Vegas, like the other tourists? You'd be broke in two days." Ian laughed. "Or were you going to take on a part-time job?" He reached out and grabbed the crotch of Jason's coveralls. "Use this not-so-little asset of yours to make a few extra credits?"

"Hardly." Jason couldn't keep the embarrassed grin off his face.

"So did you ever have an instructor tell you that whatever happens in space, stays in space?"

"Yeah."

"Well then...if you remember that saying, then you should also be able to remember that sometimes a man has to do what a man has to do." Ian pressed himself against Jason, crotch to crotch. "Join me down there for leave and I'll make sure you enjoy every last moment of your vacation."

Jason's let his mouth hang open.

· **Chapter Four**

Jason kept darting glances past the decorative patio fence at the surrounding city. He and Ian had taken seats at a patio table in one of the numerous cafés which lined the twisting streets of the city.

"You look impressed."

"It's very neat." Jason gestured with his hand. "This café—all the buildings—is just like something you'd find down on Earth. It's not what I was expecting." The architecture at least in this area of the city, was very reminiscent of the older portions of Quebec or Montreal, themselves modelled on the old villages of Europe.

Ian leaned back in his chair and laughed. "That's because you're used to only seeing the main domes. The fancy ones with their modern architecture and fancy accessories. The planners back on Earth forget that sometimes you just have to sit back and enjoy the past."

Jason looked up. High overhead he could see the curving ceiling of the triple-paned dome which enclosed the colony and kept out the Martian environment. His view of the horizon was limited—the shopping core was surrounded by apartment buildings. This was his first real view of the city. After a late-night arrival at the space port, both of them had gone directly to their hotel rooms and collapsed into their beds. *Separate beds,* Jason thought, *though we shared one room.* Nothing had happened last night, but both men had woken up with serious morning hard-ons.

Ian is really skilled with his hands, Jason thought. He could feel his dick twitching inside his jeans at the memory. *We just laid there in one bed and jerked each other off.* He looked across the table at Ian and wondered what it would be like to kiss him.

"Quebecneuve is one of the most modern and self-sustaining domes," Ian Foster explained, oblivious to Jason's line-of-thought. "It was founded more than fifty years after Earth-Dome One was erected on Mars."

Jason frowned as he crunched the math numbers in his head. "Dome One was built in Twenty-One Thirty-Four, so this city would have been built thirty years after first contact with the Dracos?"

"Yep, the foundations for the main dome were established in Twenty-Two Ninety. *Merci*," he told the waitress as she brought them their hot chocolate and pastries.

She swiped his credit-chip through a portable scanner, before returning the device to her belt. She was wearing a tight red sweater which showcased her upper chest to its best advantage, and a pair of equally snug black pants. "Call if you want anything else," she told them in a breathy, heavily-accented voice.

Jason watched her bounce her way through the tables to another pair of customers, whom she favoured with a warm smile. He looked back at Ian, who was wiping crumbs from his mouth with his paper napkin.

"It's bizarre." Jason was wearing a leather bomber jacket and jeans, and pretty much everyone else he could see was dressed equally warmly. *Now I see why Ian told me to grab all this stuff back at Yu-Wei Plex before we left.* "Why is the dome so damned cold? Is there a problem with the life support system?"

Ian threw his head back and laughed. "No, there's no mechanical problems. It's just tradition. We like to keep the weather here matching the real Quebec City."

Jason frowned at his companion. "You want to match the temperature in a self-contained dome to what the weather is like in a city back on Earth?"

"Yep."

Jason shook his head and gave a resigned laugh. "It's no wonder Marzies are looked at oddly."

"We left Earth for a place where we have to live in a sealed dome." Ian took another drink of his hot chocolate. "I think that's a sign that we were crazy to start with."

"No argument here." Jason sighed. Most domes were kept to a standard, and quite comfortable, seventy degrees. *Individual buildings and homes can be adjusted by their occupants, but the* outdoors *is always the same.* It made no sense why anyone would choose to replicate the cold winter weather here.

Ian was watching him. "No matter what planet we live on, no matter what star system we call home, we're all citizens of the Terran Colonial Union, right?"

"Mars really is an odd place."

"It attracts a certain breed of colonist. We tend to be hardy."

"I hope it's not this cold all the time." Jason drank some of his hot chocolate. "I've never liked the cold."

"The seasons match Earth. It's winter there right now."

"This is Mars...the seasons should be different."

"And maybe someday the terraforming projects will give us a vibrant world where we don't need the domes." Ian shrugged. "Right now, we do."

"So why not move to a world where you don't need a dome at all?" Jason asked. "The explorers have already found several empty ones." And the TCU had been quick to sponsor colonies on those planets, claiming them before any of the alien powers could.

"Some people are willing to colonize those *easy* worlds," Ian agreed. "Others of us like the challenge of taming Mars. A dream, for some, since the first telescopes mapped the surface."

"And thought they could see canals?" Jason laughed. "I've yet to see a canal here."

"Not enough water to waste. This is Mars, not Venice."

A young man with scraggly hair approached their table. "Either of you two fine gentlemen interested in getting really really *happy*?" he asked, nervously looking over his shoulder. "I can hook you up with just about anything." His dark coat looked grubby.

"No, thank you."

Jason nodded. "What he said."

"It's cheap, guys. I've got connections, you know."

"No, we're not interested," Ian repeated.

"Your loss then." The man turned away with a shrug, and then he hurried towards another table.

"You get that a lot here."

"At least they're polite about it." Jason finished his drink and set the mug back onto the table. He had no interest in sampling drugs. *I get my pleasures quite easily enough.* He caught himself staring at Ian.

A faint smile was playing across Ian's face.

Jason gave a start.

Ian rose to his feet. "Shall we get going then?"

"Yes, show me the sights." He stood up, giving his jacket a tug downwards to help hide the bulge in his jeans. *I never should have listened to Ian and picked out such a tight pair.* They hugged his thighs and accented his package. *People are noticing and looking.*

Ian's old pants were snug, but not as tight as Jason's.

I do like the way they hug his ass, Jason thought. *He has such a nice ass.*

They left the café and began to stroll along the street.

Jason marvelled at how quiet it was. He'd spent a lot of time in Dome-One and those streets were crowded with pedestrians and vehicles. Batteries powered electrical ones, not exhaust-spewing of course, but still there was always a lot of traffic.

"So, do you think we should try to buy terraforming equipment from one of the other races?" Jason asked, to keep the conversation going. "Or should we try to only rely on Earth-based technologies?"

"The loyal patriot part of me wants to focus on Earth," Ian admitted. "But impacting comets onto the surface to bring in more water, relying on lichens to melt the polar caps and create more atmospheric gases is a very slow process. Yes, we can terraform Mars, but it's going to take centuries and cost mega-credits."

"And if we bought technology?"

"From the Dracos?"

"Yeah."

Ian shook his head. "I think it's a bad idea to purchase too much from them. From any of the alien races actually. It will just end up costing us a lot more in the long run."

"That's my thinking too," Jason agreed. He waved his hands as he talked. "Sure, most of the aliens we've encountered are friendly enough, but our own history has shown way too many occasions when a more advanced nation has conquered and absorbed a more primitive one."

"Oh, I think the corporations can hold their own. They've been able to deal with the Dracos well enough."

"Only because the Dracos want to trade with us. I think the mega-corps are only interested in improving their own bottom lines."

"Cynic."

"Realist." Jason had no doubts that the companies would do whatever it took to gain access to alien technology in order to boost their own profits back on Earth. "We're trying too hard to catch up to the other powers."

"They're more advanced than we are. If the Dracos had been aggressive, then first contact would have gone badly for us all. Do you seriously think that the Colonial Guard could have held off an invasion fleet?"

"Not for long," Jason admitted, "but on the ground though—"

"On the ground, it would have been bloody and brutal. And we still would have lost because the aliens would have held the orbitals. They could have bombed us with complete impunity."

"Maybe...but why destroy everything you hope to conquer?"

"Who can understand the alien mind?" Ian stopped by a small booth and keyed for a copy of the newspaper.

Jason stared at the titles on display. There were several Earth-based ones, in addition to the Mars publications. "So which is better?"

Ian shrugged. "The *Daily Dome* is a more interesting read," he said, "but the *Martian Chronicle* is considered to be more accurate. That having been said, I have a definite preference for the *Weekly Mars News*, but you can't believe the page numbers in that particular rag."

ALIEN LIFE LIVING IN HYPERSPACE one headline screamed. I WAS A TAKAKAS LOVE SLAVE read another.

Jason eyed the variety of advertised papers again, then shook his head. "None of them really interest me."

"You're not much of a reader."

"Not of news, no. If I'm going to read something, I'd rather curl up with a novel. And preferably a trashy one."

"I can think of better things to curl up with."

Jason smirked. "Then let's head back to our room and see just how trashy we can be."

"Now that sounds like a plan to me!"

"I figured you'd enjoy it."

* * *

Ian swiped his key-card through the reader and door opened. He pushed Jason inside. "Are you feeling as horny as I am?" he asked.

"What do you think?" Jason replied. The front of his jeans were barely containing his throbbing hard-on. He was so hard that it actually hurt.

"Good." Ian smiled and tossed his jacket onto the floor.

Jason was smiling. He openly studied the other man's body—the way his shoulders filled out his thin cotton shirt, the shape of his back and legs, the firmness of his butt in his khaki pants.

Ian let Jason unzip and slide off his own leather jacket, then stopped him from touching the belt of his jeans. He leaned in close and kissed Jason, just a quick peck on the lips. A tease.

Jason stared back at him.

"Let me undress you," Ian said as he undid the belt and unzipped the fly. He gave Jason's erection a squeeze and the other moaned gasped. He took hold of the bottom of Jason's tee-shirt with both of his hands and slowly pulled it loose from his jeans. As he raised it, exposing Jason's stomach, he bent and began to kiss the bare flesh that emerged, sending shivers through the other man.

Jason groaned as Ian reached his nipples and took one in his mouth, flicking his tongue slowly, delicately over it until he closed my eyes and tilted his head back, his mouth opening in a soft moan of pleasure.

Ian broke off the kissing to finish lifting the tee-shirt over Jason's head. Then, he returned, softly kissing his partner's neck, chest, and nipples until Jason lost track of how many times he'd been kissed.

Ian pushed him backwards onto the bed.

Jason stared up at the ceiling as he felt his shoes and jeans being pulled off. Then Ian reached for his boxer shorts, grasping the fly with his hands and tearing them open so that his erection could burst outwards. He could feel wetness on his belly and knew that his dick must be leaking pre-cum like crazy. He hoped Ian would touch his cock with his hand or—even better—with his mouth, but instead he broke contact.

Panting softly, Jason looked up.

Ian was standing over him, smiling. "This is the first I've seen that body of yours," he announced. "You've kept it covered onboard ship."

Jason managed a shrug. "I haven't seen yours yet."

"You will." Ian bent forward and began to stroke Jason's hairy chest again.

Jason shivered in pleasure.

Ian hastily stripped off his own shirt and pants. He slid his black boxer shorts down his legs, allowing his own erect cock to stand out proudly in front of him.

Jason stared, licking his lips. *I've felt it, but now I finally get to see it.* "Damn, that's a nice sight."

Ian climbed onto the bed. "Let's fuck," he said.

"Do me."

Ian kissed Jason on the mouth again, pressing his body against the other man. Their hard cocks rubbed against each other, growing even harder.

Then Ian pulled back. "I need this so badly," he growled. "You're all mine." He tore open a small foil packet and hastily rolled the condom over his shaft.

Jason blinked. "You're gonna do that already—" He broke off with a loud gasp as Ian thrust himself forward.

"Oh yeah, you're a natural," Ian grunted.

Lying on his back with his legs spread in the air, his calves resting on his shoulders, impaled on Ian's stabbing cock, Jason reached down to grasp his own throbbing dick. He was stroking himself furiously, caught up in the moment. The sheer shock of how quickly Ian had turned dominant was a surprise, albeit an arousing one.

Ian grabbed his hands and held them down, against the bed. "No, you don't get to play like that."

"Please," Jason pleaded. "I need to cum."

There was a wicked glint in Ian's eyes. The speed of his thrusting slowed, then stopped altogether as he let the excitement and urgency which had almost carried them over the brink fade.

"Please," Jason begged. He squirmed and writhed, my sphincter muscles clenching convulsively around the other man's hard shaft. The waves of sensation created were not enough to get him off though.

"Eventually." Ian smiled down at him. "I just want to make it clear that I am still the guy in charge."

"You are, Sarge," Jason gasped. "You are!"

With another smile, Ian reached down and grabbed Jason's aching, rock-hard cock and gave it one hard, twisting stroke.

Jason gasped and reached for it himself, only to have Ian pin both of his hands to the bed again. His struggles were useless—Ian actually laughed as Jason bucked and thrashed, leaning forward so that he could not be shifted.

"That feels quite nice," he said. Then he thrust himself forward.

The sudden and hard pushed of cock into his ass made Jason cry out, shocked into ceasing his struggles.

Ian began to fall back into a rhythm again, slow at first but gradually increasing his pace until he was pounding Jason like some machine. He continued to hold Jason's hands down, not letting him touch himself until he was frantic with need, and then he finally go as he reached maximum speed.

Jason's hand darted to grasp his cock. It only took a few strokes to send himself over the edge, and he cried out incoherently as hot white jets spurted across his chest and stomach.

Ian was crying out as well, cumming inside Jason's ass.

Their cries gradually turned into harsh gasps for air.

Ian's hips began to slow their rhythm, and they collapsed into each other's arms on the bed.

Jason slumped onto the mattress. "Oh my God," he gasped.

Ian raised his head slightly and smiled tiredly at him. "I feel like I just ran a bloody half-marathon."

"You probably did, the way you were going at it."

"Shit, Jason, you've got a great ass on you. That was an amazing fuck." He slid the condom off his now-limp dick and threw it into the bathroom toilet—the small size of the hotel room made it an easy shot.

Jason groaned. "I think I pulled something." He was not used to being topped like that. He felt slimy.

"Damn," Ian continued in soft voice. "It felt so good fucking you. Your ass is just so hot and tight. Wish I'd been able to do that to you in zero-gee. Or even taken a piece of it last night."

"We were both too tired last night," Jason reminded him. *Why do I get the idea that I'm going to be walking around bow-legged for most of this vacation.* "Have you fucked a lot of guys?"

"A few. Mostly I stick with pussy."

"Ah." Jason picked up his torn boxer shorts and used them to wipe the rapidly-cooling cum from his body. *Damn, he was an animal.*

"You and I are going to have a lot of fun on this vacation," Ian told him. "We're not going back on patrol in a pent-up state."

"I'm glad to hear that."

* * *

Jason paced down the quiet street, mingling with the other pedestrians. He was feeling rather lonely. Ian had been recalled to the Yu-Wei Complex for a briefing session before the Pouncers were due to ship out again. *He wasn't expecting his vacation to be cut short like that. What could be so important?* There were plenty of security teams in the BCM who could be assigned to missions. *Why recall us?*

Two people walked passed by. "...came out from Yu-Wei," the woman was saying. Her fur-trimmed coat swirled around her legs as she walked. "They're saying that it's going to revolutionize travel."

"Yu-Wei has been working on cryotubes for decades," the man said. "Geez, Cynthia, that whole line of research was shelved after we were contacted by the Dracos. No one uses cryosleep any more."

"Not for interstellar travel, but what about terminal illness, Jacques? People who want to extend their lives? Those are the people who will be using...."

Jason stuffed his hands deeper into his jacket pockets. *Bloody cold weather...it'd be warmer outside the dome.*

Without Ian around, the French flavour of Quebecneuve lost its allure rather quickly so Jason packed up his belongings and took a tube to

Bethesda for the last three days of his vacation. His hotel room there was equally small as the one he had shared with Ian—barely larger than the single bed it contained.

Space is at a premium, he reminded himself as he walked along the corridor towards his door. *It could be worse...some apartments here are less than eight feet per wall.* The largest luxury apartments were three or four rooms with less than nine hundred square feet of space. *And people pay ten thousand credits or more a month!* It was insane.

His room was only a few feet wider than the single bed, with a private toilet and vibe-shower in an alcove. *No water showers here...too much rationing.* There were proper water showers in the truly luxury hotels and corporately-owned complexes, but he could never afford to stay there.

The comm-system was flashing.

Jason yawned. "Do I want to deal with this now?" He unzipped his jacket and tossed it onto the bed. Bethesda was still cool in temperature, but nowhere nearly as cold as Quebecneuve had been. *Damned fool idea to match winter temperatures...*

The comm-system continued flashing.

Well, I suppose I'd better watch it. At least this room has a private screen, he thought. Most hotels didn't...rooms were simply used for sleeping in and common areas provided seating and vidscreens for program viewing. "Computer, play messages."

"You have one new message," the computer informed him.

Ian's face filled the screen. "*Hi there, Jason. Hope you're enjoying your vacation while the rest of us work. Change of plans for you. Almost as bad as being in the Colonial Guard, isn't it?*" He chuckled, but his smile didn't last for long. "*Anyway, instead of meeting back at Yu-Wei Plex, you'll have to report directly to Grant's Floating Tower. Pretty fancy name for a cargo transfer station, but what can you expect for a company on the rise? We're shipping out on another patrol sooner than expected. We're leaving at fourteen fifty day after tomorrow, so if you're late, you'll have to run and catch up.*" With that he laughed again. "*See you soon. Be early and maybe we can squeeze in some pre-mission* fun." The screen went blank.

Jason sighed, but not at the change of employer. The Pouncers worked for the Belt Consortium Security Force, and were hired out to the various member corporations as needed. *We go as needed...join the Consortium and see the galaxy one cramped freighter at a time.*

· Chapter Five

The airlock doors hissed closed behind the last of the passengers as they entered the tunnel which led to their waiting shuttle.

The spaceport lounge was a fairly and austere, compared to the ports down on Earth, or even the ones at MarsDome-One. The chairs were not very comfortable; the padding was thin and the upholstery was a rough weave.

Probably chosen to be more durable than comfortable, Jason thought as he sat there. *The local authorities don't want anyone loitering here. It's arrive just in time to get on your shuttle.* He glanced towards the wall where a handful of vending machines displayed their products, but the sight took away his appetite.

At that moment, a soft chime sounded. "*Your attention please,*" an impersonal voice announced. "*Shuttle flight five seven three-delta will be delayed for approximately one hour due to routine maintenance. Thank you for your patience.*"

"Damn!"

Jason looked up from the PDA in his hand—the trashy sci-fi novel wasn't really all that interesting—to see who had spoken.

The man in question was sitting across from the check-in desk, wearing a thin white tee-shirt and body-hugging nylon track pants. His baseball cap was pushed low on his head, hiding most of his face.

He looks like a college jock, Jason thought. *Or some athlete, though why he'd be travelling on a transfer shuttle is beyond me? Tourists generally have their own shuttles; they don't take company ones.* He couldn't stop staring though.

The hunk sat on one of the hard seats, a small pack resting on the floor. He wasn't a huge guy, but he appeared to be well-built, both tall and muscled. The man shifted, raising one his arms to scratch his ear and accidentally knocked his cap back.

Oh, look at those biceps move. Jason managed to suppress a quiet sigh. *He has nice thick, dark hair. Why doesn't he leave it uncovered?* The universe wasn't fair.

The man caught Jason looking at him and he smiled.

Jason felt his heart lurch. *Wow, he's got a great smile. And nice eyes too. Real nice eyes.* Since they both seemed to be stuck on the same shuttle delay, he decided to try and spark a conversation. *I had no where else to go, right?* The shuttle port was just a small collection of low-lying buildings and landing pads outside the main dome. He could go back through the airlocks and security stations, but why waste the time?

Maybe he'll be gay and interested in popping off somewhere for a quickie? Jason dismissed the absurd thought as quickly as it had appeared. *Come on, you just had several sessions with Ian. He knows how to fuck a guy and mean it.* He gave himself a mental shake. "Hi there. Are you going to Grant's Floating Tower, too?"

The other man looked up. "Yeah, but only just long enough to catch another flight back to Earth. I'm on my way home from a little vacation."

"I'm Jason. Jason Shaw."

"Oliver Howe," the man replied and extended his large hand and firmly grasped Jason's own. "Good to meet you."

"You too. I just finished off some vacation time too. My first stay on Mars."

"It's a nice enough place, but I prefer Earth." Oliver yawned, and belatedly covered his mouth. "Sorry about that. I started out this morning at four and it's what, nearly five eight at night now? I've been in travel-tubes pretty much all day. I'm so beat." He pushed his arm up over his head, showing his sexy armpits and rippling muscles as his loose t-shirt sleeves slipped down his arms. He closed his eyes as he stretched.

Jason took the opportunity to check out his package. The crotch of his pants showed a smooth bulge. *Is he wearing a jock?* he wondered. *I do love athletic guys.* "Where were you vacationing?" he asked, hoping it would buy him some time for his own half-erect dick to soften before Oliver noticed it.

"Syra Planum," Oliver replied. "Coming to Mars was a reward from some relatives for winning the State championships."

"Nice relatives you've got. It's not a cheap flight."

"Well, it *was* the championship, right? Well, that and their twentieth wedding anniversary too. Uncle Joe and Aunt Carla live here. They miss the family, but they wanted to emigrate to Mars when they were young so up they came. They've done well with some prospecting for one of the megacorps so they had the extra money to bring some of their relatives up to visit."

"Like I said: lucky you."

"Now I have to get back home to Iowa State."

Just then, the intercom chimed. "*Your attention please. There has been a small mechanical problem found with the shuttle. Repairs are being made right now, but flight five seven three-delta will be delayed for at least two hours. Thank you for your patience.*"

"Two hours now?" Oliver groaned tiredly.

"Yeah, that's great news, isn't it? I'm getting hungry."

"Well, they have the vending machines."

"I am not eating that shit. I want something which at least *resembles* real food." Jason stood up and walked over to the desk.

The brunette gave him a friendly smile. "How can I help you, Sir?" she asked with forced politeness.

"My flight's been delayed," Jason told her. "Which I know you can't do anything about. Better to find the problem on the ground rather than blow up during the launch, right?" He gave her a friendly smile—he knew that many women considered him handsome enough, even if he wasn't interested in them. "So, given the delay is there any chance of at least getting a meal voucher for one of the star-port's kiosks?"

The brunette shook her head. "Sorry, I'm afraid I can't do that, Sir." Her computer beeped softly and she looked down. "We just received a notification that we have a priority cargo delivery for flight five seven three-delta."

"Which means?"

"We need to free up some of the passenger weight in exchange for more cargo mass. Mass equals fuel, as well as just having the physical space. If you chose to volunteer your seat, I could put you up in a hotel for the night, and then you could launch in the morning."

"And meals would be included?"

"Breakfast at least."

"That works for me." Jason smiled at her again. *I still have some vacation time left to me, after all. I'll just miss the extra* fun *with Ian, but maybe....* His eyes drifted back towards Oliver.

"Thank you, Sir. I'll just make the changes here." She swiped his identicard through the computer, and then started typing. She handed him a small card. "Your hotel voucher and changed ticket. Enjoy your flight, Sir."

"Thanks for your help." Jason walked back towards Oliver. Those beautiful eyes looked up questioningly at him. "I'm on the volunteer list," he explained. "They're going to put me up in a hotel tonight and fly me out in the morning."

"That sounds like a great idea," Oliver replied. "I should volunteer too."

Jason watched him saunter across the lounge—enjoying the view—but by the time he got to the desk five other passengers had already signed up.

Then the clerk announced another delay for the shuttle.

Oliver slumped back in his chair, flopped his legs out wide, leaned back his head and groaned.

Damn! He looks so good. Jason felt his cock harden up again as he took in the other man's closeness. He wanted to run his hands up under those clothes and feel Oliver's legs and hear Oliver make that same moan for a completely different reason.

"I'm so beat. I wish I could just go to sleep," Oliver grumbled softly.

"Well..." Jason paused as a wild idea came to him. *It probably won't work, but why not?* "I *do* have a hotel room for the night. There's no reason why we couldn't share it. Maybe you could take the morning flight, too," he suggested.

Oliver lifted his head and looked at Jason for a minute. His face broke into a wide smile, before his eyes narrowed just a bit. "You're joking."

Jason shook his head.

"Wow, that's too nice of you. I'm gonna check. Watch my stuff for me?"

"No problem." Jason got his second view of Oliver's back side and it didn't help the growing stiffness in his jeans. Oliver had nice, solid shoulders that tapered to a tight waist. His butt looked great as he strode back over to the flight check-in desk. *Damn indeed.* His *stuff* consisted of a large, green duffle bag and a smaller *Nike* bag. *He sure travels light.*

Oliver returned with that sexy smile plastered across his face. "It's done," he exclaimed as he bent down and pulled a jacket out of the *Nike* pack. He quickly donned the jacket, but left it unzipped. "This is really cool of you, dude. So let's go."

Jason picked up his own duffle and they hurried back to the travel-tube. "The hotel isn't far."

"That's good news."

The tube was fairly empty at that hour and they swiped their credit-chips at the ticket dispenser and stepped onto the platform.

A few moments later, the train arrived and the doors hissed open.

Sitting in the car, Jason's heartbeat doubled just from being near the other guy. Oliver, a laid-back guy to begin with, now relaxed totally. *My offer to share a room has turned me into a friend almost instantly, it seems.*

The ride was too short for Jason's liking, but the shuttle station was only a few minutes walk from the hotel.

"You should just wait by the elevators and I'll take care of the registration." Jason looked around the small lobby—it wasn't one of Bethesda's luxury hotels by any stretch. "I'm the one who was issued the voucher after all."

"Fine by me."

Jason walked up to the desk. "Room for one," he said offering the voucher chit to the clerk. "Shuttle delay, gotta love them, eh?" Jason kept smiling. *I'm not telling them about Oliver. I want ensure that we get just one bed in our room.*

Oliver was waiting by the elevator, holding one bag in his arm. He watched Jason walk back towards him. "Why the long face?" he asked.

"Well, I got my room but because of that voucher, and cause they don't know about you, we're gonna have to share one bed." Jason shrugged, playing his role to the hilt. "I hope you don't mind." *Make or break time.* He kept his fingers crossed.

Oliver pushed his ball cap way back on his head and it framed his smooth, sexy face. "No problem, Jason. I've been sleeping on cramped beds with two or three other guys for a month. My aunt and uncle invited a lot of company to stay at their for their anniversary and they don't have a lot of room."

Yes! Jason managed to keep the grin from his face. "We're up on the seventh floor."

"And dinner?"

"We can snag something I'm sure." Jason looked around. "There should be a dining room here. A café or something."

"Looks like the dining room is closed." Oliver had spotted the door. "There's a take-out bar at least."

"Not quite what I had in mind, but it will do." Jason checked out the selections in their bins. "Not much better looking than what the spaceport had. Hopefully it tastes better." He selected a fish burger and fries—it smelled like fish at least.

Oliver grabbed a bagel and a carton of milk.

"Is that all you want?"

"I'm not all that hungry," he replied.

After eating their meal, Jason led Oliver up to their room. "Well, here it is." He swiped his key-card through the lock and the door opened. The room was typically small for Mars. It had one average-sized bed, with barely two feet of clearance around it. "Cozy." He pulled off his leather jacket and hung it on a hook.

Oliver immediately threw his duffle on the floor and began to rustle inside it. "I'm gonna clean up a little. Need to use the can?"

"No, I'm good for now."

"Okay." Oliver undid the Velcro on his sneakers, pulling them off and then padded into the suite's tiny bathroom.

Jason sat on the edge of the bed and tried to calm down while Oliver brushed his teeth and cleaned up. *I want to have Oliver's moans fill this room and I want to be the person who causes them,* he thought. *I hope I didn't misjudge him.* Jason thought about how to start things.

He considered just sliding his hands *accidentally* into Oliver's crotch when they got into bed. *Or maybe I should just jump him outright.*

Oliver emerged from the bathroom before Jason could come up with a plan. He had stripped off his jacket and shirt and the sight of his chest almost took Jason's breath away. He had exactly the kind of build Jason loved. High, tight pecs, with a long, muscular torso. His abs were as tight, flat and hard as the coverboy on a men's health magazines. He had a nice amount of black hair in the centre of his chest and a sexy shading at the base of his abs.

Jason tried not to simply stand and stare.

"Oh, man." Oliver stretched out his arms. "I'm going straight under the covers. I hope you don't want to watch the 'casts or anything, Jason?"

"No, nothing good on." *Everything I want to see is right here.* "I'm tired out too."

"Good." Oliver reached up and pulled his track pants down, revealing a snug, dark blue pair of bikini briefs that cupped his nice bulge.

Jason felt his knees almost give way. *It's not a jock strap, but oh do those briefs ever look good with his tanned skin and black hair.*

Oliver pulled down the blankets and slid himself into the bed.

Jason hastily hopped into the vibe-shower for the minute or so it took to get cleaned up. The tiny bathroom had a toilet and a metered spigot for drinking water.

Jason kept his boxer shorts and tee-shirt on, just to try and help hide his raging hard-on. *I want to feel his chest next to mine but I might lose my load if it happens,* he thought.

Oliver lay on his back, one sheet intersecting his abdomen and part of his briefs. He had one arm behind his head, exposing lots of black curly hair in his armpits.

"Lights down!" Jason called out, then carefully slid into bed next to him.

Oliver sighed contentedly as the room darkened for sleeping—there was just enough ambient light to make out shadow shapes. "Dude, this was really a great move. I'd never have of thought of it."

Jason turned my head and looked into the other man's eyes, now just inches away. "Hey, Oliver. I'm glad it worked out as well. I'm traveling alone and you're proving to be very good company."

He smiled back. "So, Jason, I didn't ask, but are you seeing anybody special?"

"No. I'm just finishing my own vacation and heading back to work. You're not, uh, married, right?"

"Nope. Single and available," Oliver replied. He closed his eyes but Jason could tell he wasn't asleep.

Jason looked at his profile in the darkened room. Then Oliver moved, turning onto his side so he was facing towards Jason.

Jason didn't dare move.

"So Jason, do you have a girlfriend?"

Caught off-guard, Jason paused for way too long, but finally decided to be honest. "Nope, no girlfriend."

Oliver lay in silence for quite a bit. "How about a boyfriend then?" he asked softly.

Jason looked over and he could tell that Oliver's eyes were open. They sparkled even in the near darkness. "Uh, well," he stammered. "Actually, uh, not—not right now."

"You're gay, aren't you?"

Jason stopped breathing for a minute. The situation with this guy was moving faster than he even fantasized. *What's he gonna do if I come out to him?* he wondered. *I don't think he'd freak out though. He seems way too laid back. And he did ask.* Jason turned his head toward the other man and just nodded.

Oliver's smile grew a bit more. "I knew it."

"How?" Jason demanded.

"Well, I saw how you were looking at me back in the spaceport and on the tube. I've seen it before. I know I'm in pretty good shape and I've seen a lot of guys look at me like that. Plus, I'm getting some good vibes off you."

Jason nodded his head rather slowly. "I see. Does this worry you? I mean, sharing a bed and all?"

"No."

"You're not—"

"No, I'm not."

Jason felt a surge of disappointment, then he gave himself a shake. *Don't be so silly,* he told himself. *What were the odds of him being gay? Just because I want to mess around with him so badly...* "Well, don't worry, I—"

Oliver cut him off. "But I've always been curious."

Jason's felt his mouth drop open. *The next few moments are going to decide the course of the whole evening. What the hell do I say now?* His mind, caught up in both lust and Oliver's manly aroma, just couldn't work very fast. "Oliver, I really didn't invite you to share a room just so I could jump you. Yeah, you're really hunky, but I'm not gonna force myself onto you."

Oliver had turned over and lay on his back now, staring up at the tan ceiling tiles. "I've been wrestling since I was eleven," he said. "I've had a few guys grope me in matches and I even kinda messed around with one guy on the team. But I never could let anything happen back home. There was just too much risk of it going badly and messing things up. Some small-town attitudes haven't changed in two hundred years."

He turned his head to face Jason. "But I feel really relaxed with you. I barely know you, but I'm totally comfortable being around you. And...well, I was just wondering, if you could...show me...."

Jason stared right back at him.

Oliver glanced at him nervously, but then he relaxed as a goofy-looking grin spread across Jason's face. He responded with his own nervous grin. "Jason, I *want* to do this. You're turning me on like you just wouldn't believe."

Jason smiled even more. "Really?"

"Yep."

That turned him on even more. *I know I have a good build, given the demands of my job, but really.* He decided to begin the plunge. *Looks like I'm gonna be the teacher.* With that thought, he placed his hands on Oliver's chest. The feel of his warm, smooth skin made him moan just a bit and he felt his body tighten as he made contact. "Oliver, I want you to turn over on your stomach. We'll only go as far as you want. Anytime you want to stop, say so. It's your show."

Oliver looked back at him. "Do it." Then he closed his eyes, nodded once, and turned on his stomach.

· **Chapter Six**

Jason pulled the pillows out of the way, and pushed the sheet down off both their bodies. He could feel the heat rising off Oliver. He quickly yanked off his tee-shirt and tossed it onto the floor. "I'm going to start with a simple massage. You just relax and let me know how it feels. Is it okay if I straddle you?"

"Yeah," Oliver told him. "Do what you want."

Jason settled onto his body, kneeling just below the other man's brief-covered butt. "Push your arms out to the sides," he ordered, and then he began rubbing Oliver's muscular shoulders. *His skin is so tan and smooth.* He had virtually no hair on his back, except for a dusting just above the waistband of his tight briefs.

Jason suppressed a groan. *I don't know if he can feel my hard-on or not, but I doubt an iron rod could be any stiffer than my cock right now. Good thing I've still got my boxers on.* As he ran his hands down Oliver's shoulder-blades, the other man let out a tiny moan. "Oliver, if it feels good, let me know. It also turns me on." Jason began lightly running his fingers up along his spine, and Oliver let out a long, moan.

"Oh, Jason. That's really good."

Jason's hands touched every inch of Oliver's back. He leaned forward as he rubbed those shoulders again and breathed in the smell of his skin. It smelled sweet, warm and slightly perfumed, like he had used talcum power on it. *I just want to kiss and lick that back of yours,* he thought, *but first things first. No need to rush things.*

Oliver shifted down as Jason's hands pressed and massaged his lower back. Oliver moved his legs a bit, causing his ass to pump up, first one cheek, then the other.

I hope those hairs continue all the way down. Jason's hands skimmed along the top of his bikini briefs and he carefully allowed one of his fingers to slip under the waistband for just a second.

Oliver moaned softly.

Jason shifted himself lower, and quickly brushed his hands over Oliver's ass-cheeks. The briefs felt solid and packed. Oliver's thighs were magnificent, and his sexy black hairs tickled Jason's fingers as he kneaded the back of his legs. Jason made his hand into a fist and ran it along the outside of his leg, pushing the muscles down.

"Oh, that feels so nice."

Jason could see just how much Oliver had relaxed. He had one arm along his side, the other straight out. His legs were spread open and his head was turned to the side. "Glad you're enjoying yourself." He moved down to Oliver's feet, and lifted his calf as he massaged each toe, then ran his hand up and down, from Oliver's knee to his ankle. Then, with a grin, he leaned down and blew softly on the back of his knee.

Oliver's soft moans filled the tiny room. He made the sound Jason had first heard in the star-port.

This time, it was *in response to my touch.* Jason was in heaven as his young hunk switched his head to the other side and lifted his midsection and ass up off the bed for a moment. Jason ran his hands lightly up the inside of Oliver's strong legs, almost touching the bulge of his balls, cupped and hidden within those tight blue briefs.

Oliver inhaled sharply at the touch.

"I think it's time to finishing undressing you. No, don't move. Let me do it." Jason leaned forward on his hands, and slid his thighs along Oliver's warm, hairy legs.

Oliver tensed as Jason's weight momentarily pressed down on him—Jason's hard-on was unmistakable against his back—but he offered no protest.

Jason slid his hands along Oliver's arms and moved his face right to the back of his head. He slid the rest of his body up until all of his body was laying atop his new buddy. Jason's hard cock, still wrapped in his boxer shorts, bulged out and slid into the space between Oliver's cheeks. Jason wiggled his hips and Oliver responded by moving his ass up and down. *It was almost tentative,* Jason thought. *I wonder if he's really is sure just how far he wants to go?* "How's that feel?"

"Good. I love having your body on top of me. I can feel your hard-on."

"It's all because of you," Jason told him. "You are just too hunky." He slid his hands along his sides, up and down, then lifted his body up.

Oliver shifted again, flexing both of his cheeks under the bikini briefs.

Shit, I need to see you totally nude. Jason reached out with his hand and slowly traced a few figure eights along Oliver's lower back.

Oliver had stopped even attempting to speak.

Jason loved the chorus of moans he was inciting from the other man—his own erection throbbed in matching pulses. He slipped his finger back under the soft cotton fabric of those briefs, just for a moment, feeling the warmth envelop his finger and the tickle of many hairs on his fingertip.

Then he slid that single finger along Oliver's tight cheeks, rubbing firmly on his still-covered ass.

"Unnhh," Oliver moaned. "Oh, Jason, that's so good."

"I want to see your ass, Oliver. Can I?"

"Fuck yeah! Dude, you are making me feel so...damn! Do whatever you want."

With his face just inches from Oliver's butt, Jason put two fingers inside each side of his underwear and pulled them down. He could see a light dusting of hair which covered Oliver's body, thickening as it led between his cheeks.

Jason leaned forward. *He smells so nice and clean.* He moved his tongue over the exposed ass. The boy was moaning almost continuously now. Jason slowly worked his way lower. He planted soft kisses on one cheek, then the other. Slowly, he eased Oliver's briefs down even further. Now half of his ass was visible. He ran his hands down Oliver's legs again, then back up to those nice cheeks. One more tug and his entire ass lay exposed.

Jason moved closer, positioning himself so that Oliver's tight legs cradled his torso, and his hands were free to touch his back, butt, and upper thighs. Jason rubbed his hot skin as he kissed and licked first one side of his ass, then the other.

Oliver was built much lean and long.

Jason was grinning. *I don't have to ask…no one has ever done this to him before.* Softly, he breathed into those dense, black hairs in the centre of his butt. He put both hands right on the high, muscular tops of his ass and spread Oliver's cheeks just a bit. As he leaned forward, Oliver's groans got louder. Jason blew once more, then extended his tongue and quickly flicked it back and forth. Another breath, another lick, closer and closer, sometimes high, sometimes low. He couldn't see Oliver's cock at all because those blue bikini briefs still covered that part of him. *But I know he's hard.* Especially when he zeroed in on the centre of his ass. He smelled clean and smoky at the same time. As his tongue wormed through the moist, dark hairs and touched the outside of his hole, Oliver began moaning Jason's name over and over, too.

Jason kept licking him, tasting him, feeling his hard muscles ripple as Oliver moved his ass up and down and tried to turn his head from one side to the other. Finally, he let up and Oliver groaned and lay still. Small beads of sweat glistened in the centre of his back.

"Oh my God, Jason. What were you doing? I've never felt so much intense feeling in my life. That was…wonderful."

Jason didn't say anything for a moment He looked at Oliver's thick, full hair on the back of his head, the wide, brown shoulders, the way his back tapered down to his firm, tight waist, with those two white cheeks exposed and framed by his underwear, and his long, tough legs. "If it's too much, we can stop," he teased.

"No! Shit! It's just all so new. I've never had anyone do that to me before. It was amazing."

"I kinda figured as much."

Oliver smiled into the pillow, his eyes still closed.

He looks rested. Jason began running his hand in circles on Oliver's back, warming him up again. *His skin feels so smooth.* He concentrated on his sides, feeling his arms and the sides of his ribcage. He moved gently over this sensitive area as Oliver twitched and jerked slightly.

Jason got up on his hands and knees, still bent over Oliver, and began working his hand underneath his body. Oliver shifted his torso a bit to give him some room, but Jason didn't want him turning over, yet. "Don't roll over. I want to touch first," he whispered. "I'll have plenty of time to look, later." *As handsome and built as he looks from this side, I can't wait to see what he's packing. I've never been a size queen, but I have a feeling that Oliver's will be just like his long, firm, build.*

Jason worked his hand along his abs. This is probably his second most favourite part of a man's body.

Oliver didn't have abs of marble, but his waist felt tight, hard and flat.

Jason spread his hand out wide and pushed his fingers along Oliver's body. He moved his hand down and brushed along the hairs around his belly button. His briefs had hitched down a bit, exposing some pubic hair and he pushed his fingers back and forth through it. It felt thick and silky at the same time, and slightly moist from all the activity on the other side of his body. He moved further down and touched a hard lump covered in soft cotton.

Oliver erased any doubts about what he was feeling when his moans picked up in intensity and his moans acted like a homing beacon for Jason, guiding him to the places he loved the best.

"Oliver, it's time to turn over." Jason paused while Oliver obeyed. "Now just close your eyes, push your arms out to the sides, and relax." He could not help but stare.

Oliver looked magnificent. His tight blue briefs held his bulging cock against his abdomen. He had well-defined abs, a light tracing of black hairs in the middle of his chest, with more dark tufts under each arm.

Moving his own body over Oliver's legs once more, Jason began massaging the other man's shoulders. *I'm moving way too fast,* he thought, but he could barely keep himself from bringing his lips toward Oliver's full, ripe mouth. *I bet he's had plenty of kissing experience.* Jason rubbed Oliver's chest and he let one fingernail tease a nipple.

Oliver grunted. "Oh, wow. That feels great."

"You mean...this?" Jason asked as he flicked his other nipple.

"Yessss. Oh, nice."

"You have sensitive nipples, Oliver? Do you like it when I play with them?"

"Yeah. I do it once in a while, when I beat off."

Grinning, Jason flicked his finger rapidly back and forth over one, then the other. Both actions brought a full, deep moan from Oliver. And as he glanced down, Jason could see that the bulge in his own boxer shorts hadn't changed a bit. He moved down toward Oliver's crotch, intent now on finally unveiling his cock. He rubbed his hand over the cotton, smoothing the bulging bikinis.

Jason slid down the bed a bit more, and leaned into Oliver's crotch. He let his face press against the material, feeling the hard flesh twitch as he touched it. He slipped his fingers under the briefs and smoothly pulled them down.

Oliver's cock looked every bit as magnificent as the rest of his body. He was about seven inches, average thickness, and framed in a mass of dark, shiny pubic hair.

Jason watched it pulse as he anticipated what was going to be a very long, wet, and exciting blow job. For both of them.

Jason stared down at the other man, laying there, arms spread, totally nude, eyes closed, so lean and sexy, with his dick as hard as a rock. He leaned forward and blew a soft stream of air up and down the length of the shaft.

"Uh...oh God, Jason," Oliver moaned. "I...I...man, just do it."

"Do what?" Jason teased.

"Please!" Oliver pleaded more forcefully, but with a small smile on his face. He leaned his head forward and fixed his dark eyes onto Jason. "Suck me."

"Oh, I will, Oliver. But I want to do something else, first. You just lay back, relax, and let me know how it feels."

He moved forward on the bed, stretching out until his head came even with Oliver's. He laid on his side, resting his head on one hand. With the other, he traced a pattern over Oliver's pecks, his nipple, those firm abs, and then slowly down into his pubic hair. "Hey, no peeking," he warned as Oliver's eyes began to open. "Just lay back and feel it."

Oliver smiled, shook his head slightly, and lay back down. His abs had flexed as his head lifted and when he relaxed, the muscles smoothed out once again.

Jason's right hand and slowly encircled Oliver's cock. Gently, he began stroking, up and down. Oliver turned his head to one side, then the other as Jason's fingers moved up and down his cock. His thick cock fit into Jason's hand so well, and it was just long enough to let him move his hand up about a hand-length, then back down.

"Jason," he said breathily as Jason settled into a rhythm.

"Yes, Oliver?"

"It...feels...great."

"Mmm. I'm glad."

"You can't keep this up, though, man."

"Why not, Oliver?" he said, stroking the warm shaft, up and down.

"Be-because." Oliver's body began revealing the pleasure it was feeling from his hand. Every few moments a tremor would move through him as the sensations traveled to every part of his hunky body. "Oh, stop."

Jason grinned at the desperate moan. *I don't want to make him cum this way, but I'm willing to push it. Because I don't know him very well.*

I don't know when he's getting too close, but I certainly don't think it will necessarily end the evening if it happens. "Why should I stop?"

"Because I'll shoot. I've never had anyone beat me off. Oh, God!" Another tremor moved through his body. "Jason, c'mon, I'm getting close...."

Jason leaned forward, still stroking him, and moved his lips to Oliver's nipple. He stuck out his tongue and flicked it back and forth, back and forth, causing the tit to harden and poke out of those solid pecks.

"Ah, yes. Wow, man oh, yeah," Oliver said, moving his head from side to side. He moved one hand toward his dick, motioning like he wanted to take over the masturbation, but Jason released his penis and pushed his hand away.

"No cheating."

"Aw, you're killing me. You get me close but not close enough."

"Maybe that's the idea," Jason replied. "Just go with it."

Oliver laid his hand back down. He lifted his hips a bit and Jason kept a solid grip on his cock, but didn't let all of his fingers touch him at one time. His penis was like a bar of curved steel. His thigh muscles bulged as the stroking continued.

Jason was enjoying this immensely. He loved watching Oliver's legs flex and move under their dust of black hairs. His own cock was ready to blow, too, just looking at that hot body. He knew that when it was his turn, he probably wouldn't be able to last as long as Oliver.

Jason pulled Oliver's cock away from his body, then let it thump back against his body. His balls, nestled in his shiny black pubic hair, seemed tight. *That*, he knew, *is a dangerous sign*. He resumed his steady stroking.

Oliver spread his arms out to both sides of the bed, seemingly steadying himself before each wave of feeling raced up and down his lean, tight body. "Jason!"

"Yeah?"

"I'm getting close. Really, I'm going to shoot. You're stroking me...it feels so good. Please, let me cum, Jason."

As soon as he said that, Jason slowed down his strokes. *Is he getting even thicker?* Was that possible? "I want to keep this going for a lot longer." It *was* harder to wrap his hand around it. "I want you to do something first, Oliver," he said softly.

"What? Tell me."

"I want you to get up on your hands and knees."

Oliver hardly paused. His muscled stomach rippled as he lifted himself to a sitting position. He wrinkled the forehead of his handsome face, his gorgeous eyes full of passion and a question.

"Just do it. This will be so good, Oliver."

As Oliver turned onto his hands and knees, Jason sat back and looked at him from behind. His cheeks flexed with solid muscle, two huge dimples on each side. He didn't have a large bubble butt, but instead had a lean, muscular ass that fit so well with his lean, hunky body. His hard-on throbbed as he took in those tight calves, the strong thighs and the dramatic taper from his narrow waist to his broad, sexy shoulders. Jason hastily moved to the head of the bed, and slid around to his back. "Move over, Oliver. I want you to fuck my mouth."

Oliver's eyes widened slightly, either with surprise or excitement. He quickly moved his legs tightly together and he swung one leg over, straddling Jason with his body. "Like this?"

"Yep." Jason ran his hands from Oliver's bulging shoulders, down his torso, and then along his thighs. "I want to suck your cock and when you get close, I want you to shoot it all over my chest, okay?"

"Yep." Oliver nodded as he moved his thick cock toward Jason's mouth. He felt Jason's hands reach his ass and his heartbeat picked up a beat or two as those fingers ran lightly over the warm, sexy cheeks and pulled him closer.

Jason's right hand reached for Oliver's cock. It bobbed in the air, still arching toward its owner's flat, hard abs, and he grabbed the cut head and gently tugged. Oliver stretched his torso out and let himself be guided down toward the watering mouth.

Even then Jason felt the urge to tease him just a little. He ran his nose along the side of the thick cock, down to the black, wiry pubic hair, inhaling his wonderful scent. One hand ran along Oliver's balls while the other still rested on his ass. Oliver's chest filled his vision as he lowered his body closer. He moved his legs, feeling their hairy thighs tickle. Slowly Jason rubbed his face along Oliver's cock, making it jump up and down. He turned his head slightly to the side and rubbed his cheek along his rock hard abs. He felt the heat of Oliver's body all over his face and he could hear the soft grunts as the other man kept flexing his body, aiming his penis at his mouth.

"Now." He lay back, pulled Oliver forward with a strong tug, and let him drive his hard cock into his hot, warm mouth. His vision was filled with abdomen, cock, and pubic hair. He felt almost as if he was completely surrounded by Oliver.

Oliver's big strong cock moved in and out of his mouth, slowly at first as he slowly measured how deeply he could go.

Jason moved his hand from Oliver's ass to his arm, finding a bulging mound of solid bicep. He kept his hand there, feeling the muscular arm pump as he lowered down and up, down and up. He kept his lips tight around the man's cock, rolling his tongue along the underside. It tasted hot, smoky and sexy. This guy was one of the hottest guys he had ever been with. He wanted to bring him off, but he also didn't want the session to end.

Oliver began lengthening his slide in and out. His strong thrusts pushed Jason's head flat against the pillow. He felt Jason relaxed and finally allow him to set the pace. He kept thrusting his hips, sliding his cock slid in, and then sliding it back out, until the head just cleared Jason's eager lips. Once or twice he would pull out too far and his cock would pop out, bouncing wetly against his stomach. But he would quickly move his hips down and forward in a push for that waiting mouth. "Oh, Jason. This is so good. I've never fucked anyone's mouth. Where....unnhh....don't, don't stop, man."

Jason didn't have much say in the matter as Oliver continued to flex his strong muscles, pushing his hard shaft into his mouth. He slid his hand to Oliver's waist. He wasn't sure how Oliver reacted when he got close, so he tried to listen to the other man's breathing. *Wow, is his cock ever thick and rigid. It's throbbing. And boy does that turn me on.* Jason moved his other hand down to his own hard-on and began stroking. *It won't take long for me. I feel so very close.*

Oliver began to make small noises—quick intakes of breath as Jason's tongue rubbed along that sensitive spot just under the head of his cock. He seemed on autopilot now.

Jason couldn't see Oliver's face but he settled in a steady pace, moving that hard-on in and out of his mouth. He felt Oliver's quick intakes of breath as bursts of pleasure raced up and down his body from his sucking. Through the hand on his waist, he began to feel Oliver tightening up. His hunky star-port jock was going to shoot—and shoot soon. Jason wanted to time things so they would come as close together as he could arrange.

"Unhh, yeah. I'm so close, I'm getting close, Jason. Oh, oh, oh," Oliver said softly, the passion evident in his voice. In and out, in and out, his cock plunged deep into that eager mouth and Jason sucked harder. "Oh, I'm gonna blow. I'm gonna cum!"

Jason kept jacking himself, but moved his hand to Oliver's flat stomach and gently pushed, hoping the hunk wasn't too lost in the feelings to remember to pull out.

Suddenly, Oliver pulled back and dropped to one knee, keeping the other one up to brace himself. He squeezed his nipple with his left hand right, and put the other onto his cock, jacking it off. "Here it comes," he gasped tightly as it started.

Jason felt the first warm contact against the side of his face. Oliver's cum literally exploded out of his cock like a WebCaster blob, his body arching as the feelings took over and that sight sent Jason over the edge, too. "Oliver, I'm going cumming too!" As blasts of Oliver's hot cum splashed on his chest and visions of his muscled, sexy body filled his eyes, he felt himself begin to explode. The feelings felt incredibly intense and they went on for what seemed like a very, very long time.

Both men moaned loudly as their orgasms slowly faded.

Oliver lowered himself on his side, as he finished shooting his load. He whipped his head back and forth as the feelings moved up and down his body. As they subsided, Oliver rolled over, bringing his chest into contact with Jason's, mingling their cum together. He moved forward until their lips touched and they kissed.

Jason moved his hand to Oliver's back and pulled him tight. They were both pretty sticky, but oh did it feel fabulous.

Oliver ran one hand through his jet black hair as he broke the kiss and nestled alongside me. "Dude, that was...great," he said with a completely contented sigh.

Jason felt the warm body relax alongside him. He laid still for a moment, feeling Oliver's torso, and feeling his own heartbeat begin to return to normal. *I'm not about to move,* he thought. He pulled up the sheet to cover them both before drifting into a deep and very sound sleep.

· **Chapter Seven**

Jason stepped into the small lounge, enjoying the luxury of being able to walk in normal gravity. *Or least the artificial approximation of Earth normal gravity.* The room was typical for one of the corporations—plain walls painted a pale pastel green colour, with floor tiles buffed to a bright sheen. The rectangular conference table was wood—possibly solid hardwood, more likely just veneered—and the dozen chairs around it had matching leather upholstery. The rest of the Pouncers were already seated around the table, most with coffee mugs in front of them.

"About time you got here," Ian grumbled from where he was standing to one side of the room. He was wearing his regular duty uniform. No sidearm, or other weaponry, of course, but his coveralls were freshly cleaned and pressed.

Out to impress someone, are we? Jason was also wearing the standard crimson and brown uniform. He'd found time to change into it after his shuttle had docked with the station. *Just enough time to dash to my quarters, change clothes, and then find my way here.* "My original shuttle got cancelled."

"Sure it was."

"I had to reschedule to a flight the next day."

"How convenient for you."

"You want to call Bethesda dome and check on me?"

"Maybe I should."

"I made it to this meeting on time, didn't I?" Jason demanded. *And only just...the morning shuttle was scheduled to launch a lot later than I'd expected it to be.* But then, he and Oliver had spent that much more time in bed together. *I'm gonna be stiff for a week,* he thought to himself. *If anything, he was even hornier and more eager after sleeping. Gave him a taste of man-to-man action one night and the next morning he wakes up as a total cock-hound.*

Ian was still glaring at him. "You could have commed me at least."

"I never thought about it," Jason admitted, somewhat sheepishly. "I was waiting for the shuttle and it kept getting delayed with mechanical problems. When the clerk finally offered me a hotel room for the night, I was so ready for bed that I never thought of calling you." *That and that fact that I was busy fucking a hunky guy I'd just met.*

"Well next time I'm waiting for you, you damn well better have the decency to call!"

"Are you two lovebirds done?" Franco asked in too-sweet voice from the chair he was seated in.

Jason felt his face flush as Brad's laughter echoed too loudly.

Ian grimaced, but he made no reply. He left Jason and paced over to a refreshment station to get himself another mug of coffee.

Damian Bowie caught Jason's eye and he simply waved at the chair beside him.

Jason sauntered over to the empty chair and sat down with a tired groan. The chair felt quite comfortable though.

"Rough night?"

"What?"

"You look tired," Damian told him.

"Just jet-lag," Jason replied. "Too much travelling I guess."

"Yeah, that extra half-hour sleeping time on Mars takes some getting used too."

"Oh yeah." Jason had forgotten than the day on Mars was half an hour longer than Terran Standard. The Martians added that time between three and four, and slept through it.

Damian gave him a grin.

Terry and Joshua were talking softly to one another.

The door hissed open and a well-dressed Asian businessman stepped through it. He paused to give the squad a careful, studying look. "Gentlemen, it is good to see that you are all prompt." His English was lightly accented. "That augers well for a successful round of negotiations." He had a receding hairline, and an equally prominent paunch. His dark purple tie was bright against his powder blue shirt and black suit jacket.

Ian hastily took his seat at the table, watching the man pause long enough to pour himself a mug of coffee and then take the chair at the head of the table. "Well, Mister Takashima?"

"Well indeed, Sergeant Foster."

Ian nodded to him.

Jason tried to pay attention—the man's tailored suit looked like it cost more credits than he'd earn in a decade. *So who is this? And how does Ian know him?*

Takashima studied them all one more time and then he nodded his head as he came to a decision. "I shall be brief then." He remote-locked the door and then inserted a data-crystal into the slot on the tabletop. "I represent the Yu-Wei Company."

Terry whistled softly.

Jason blinked. *That's one of the biggest corporations around. They have satellite facilities in almost every star system the TCU controls.* He frowned. *We are playing with the big boys now.*

Takashima continued talking. "We have acquired your services for a period of time to provide security for one of our operations. We do not normally bother outsourcing such employment opportunities, but given the increasing nature of the interconnectedness of Belt Consortium members, we are making the effort." He paused for a moment. "Do not think that our own corporate security is lacking in any way."

"That thought never crossed any of our minds, Mister Takashima." Ian kept a warm, pleasant tone in his voice.

"Your squad has been highly recommended to us by your superiors. You will find that your pay rates are well within Consortium standards. The chance of earning bonus pay is minimal, but should you engage in combat, you will be fully compensated."

"So what's the duty gonna be?" Franco asked. "Freighter guard?"

"Outpost security." Takashima looked at him. "Yu-Wei maintains a small, though quite profitable, mining operation on Saturn VI. The moon is more popularly known as *Titan*. You will be going there."

Jason frowned. "Way out there?"

"Yes, Mister Shaw, all the way out there."

"What do you mine?" Joshua asked.

"Hydrocarbons."

Joshua frowned.

"Oil and gas," Damian whispered to him.

"Oh."

Takashima gestured and a hologram of Titan wavered into life over the table. "Since the Cassini probes first visited that moon back in the early two thousands, we have known that Titan has hundreds of times more liquid hydrocarbons than all the known oil and natural gas reserves on Earth. These hydrocarbons simply rain down from the sky, collecting in vast deposits, which form the hundreds of lakes you can plainly see. Any single one of those lakes is estimated to contain more hydrocarbon liquid than any of Earth's current oil and gas reserves."

Franco yawned.

Takashima frowned and Ian looked annoyed.

"There are several mining concerns out there," Damian said. "Opening up the moon to exploration was a popular decision by EarthGov."

"Yes, there are several companies operating there. Most of them are concentrated in the northern latitudes." Several icons flashed on the holo-map, showing those operations. Takashima cleared his throat. "Right now, our facility—it's been named Titan-Trove by the previous administrator—is located in the *southern* latitudes." Another icon flashed. "The research team is getting close to a significant breakthrough in mining techniques and the company wants to increase its security there."

"What type of breakthrough?" Damian asked.

"That is information, sadly, is classified."

Ian grimaced.

"So we have go to Saturn and stand watch over a bunch of eggheads?" Franco grumbled. "All that way for surface duty? What's the risk?"

"All of the other mining operations are run by rival companies...despite the benefits of the alliance which is the Belt Consortium, we are all still out to make individual profits. And the non-members are equally eager to steal marketshare from us."

Jason shook his head. *I never cared for the corporate ideals.*

"There is a considerable rivalry among all companies. Any one of them would very happily sabotage or destroy a rival's facility in order to gain greater profitability. Even with the rest of the galaxy opening up to exploration, the resources of the solar system are still worth exploiting. And possibly open warfare."

"Corporate warfare."

"Yes, Sergeant Foster. The Colonial Guard manages to keep a lid on the worst of the piracy and territorial disputes, but their warships cannot be everywhere. Not every hijacker is truly an independant pirate. Many are privately sponsored by a corporation seeking an advantage over its rivals."

"Does Yu-Wei sponsor pirates?" Brad asked.

Takashima looked offended by the question.

"Private Kellar, Yu-Wei is a law-abiding company," Ian snapped. "That question is completely uncalled for."

Brad looked embarrased.

Jason frowned. *I don't see Takashima denying it though.* Of course, the executive might truly not know if his corporation was making use of pirates. *Or would they more accurately be considered privateers,* he wondered.

"This is going to be a simple operation of us moving in to guard the facility. Buildings, equipment, and personnel." Ian eyed his squad. "Nothing different than any other BCM-dictated operation."

"We're just gonna guard your miners?"

"Mining on Titan is not easily accomplished." Takashima took a sip of his coffee. "The average temperatures are one hundred and fifty below and the atmosphere is rich in highly flammable elements."

"The hydrocarbons."

"Precisely. A small mistake in setting mining charges can result in catastrophic explosions." A quick smile darted across Takashima's face. "We have been fortunate thus far, but Exxon lost an entire survey crew just last month."

Damian swallowed loudly.

Jason glanced at him.

"Our breakthrough in mining techniques could be worth billions, once we patent the process. The other companies know that we are getting close and the risk of espionage is high. We simply need to ensure facility security until that time."

"In any event, that's our assignment," Ian told his squad. "If anyone has objections, now is the time to voice them."

No one said anything.

Takashima gave Ian a nod.

"Any questions?"

"Titan has a gravity of point fourteen Earth normal."

Terry frowned. "So what, Damian? You just showing off?"

"I'm just pointing that out. We just came off a zero-gee patrol. I thought policy was that we spent time in three-quarter to full Earth normal."

"It's less than Luna." Joshua grimaced and shook his head. "I spent some time there once. I didn't like it."

"Deal with it," Ian told him. "Policy changes as per the dictates of our supervisors. It was a short patrol on the *Reckoning,* so there's no risk of muscle/bone degradation. Just take your pills and spend time in the gym as per procedure. Right now, we are going to Titan."

Ian paused. "Titan's atmosphere has a surface pressure more than one and a half times that of Earth, like being five metres underwater if you're into swimming and diving. The air is ninety-eight per cent nitrogen, with a lot of other trace gases. Most of them poisonous. Some, like Mister Takashima said, are flammable. It'll be a balmy minus one hundred and seventy degrees on average. If we venture outside of the colony, it will require us to wear full environmental suits."

"Oh goody." There was no mistaking the heavy sarcasm in Franco's voice.

Jason shook his head. "Another vacation spot."

Ian grimaced. "You lot want to spend time on exotic worlds? Then go and join the Colonial Guard."

Takashima gave Ian a look, his eyes narrowing. "Your squad accepts the posting?"

"We do." Ian gave the Squad's verbal consent, even though both men knew that the upper echelons of the Belt Consortium Militia had already agreed to it. This briefing was really just a formality for the Pouncers.

"Excellent news." Takashima managed to sound pleased by the agreement, as if negotations had really been much more difficult. "Then you will all receive your full documentation shortly, along with your first payment."

Ian nodded.

"Yu-Wei will supply you with transportation aboard one of our private *Mediator* carriers. The *Watchful Eye* will be leaving port in thirty-one hours, escorting a freighter convoy to Titan. Your service will begin en route—you will supplement shipboard security until the convoy reaches Titan. You will be shuttled down to the surface and your tour will last a minimum of five months...and then we shall examine your contracts for possible extension."

"That sounds acceptable." Ian paused. "Any other questions? No, dismissed."

The squad rose to their feet.

Ian gestured towards Jason. "Want to stay behind, Corporal Shaw?"

"Do we have something talk about?" Jason asked him. The room was empty now—everyone else had left, and the cleaning staff had not arrived.

"Your attitude has gone downhill."

"I'm just tired."

"You seemed fine in Quebecnouvelle."

"That was when we were on vacation. We're back on duty now. Sir."

Ian's eyes narrowed. "Then I should let you get back to your quarters and pack for the trip. Dismissed."

* * *

Jason picked idly at the limp noodles on his plate. The sauce was far more bland than he had expected it to be. *I had such high hopes for this meal too.*

"You want to talk about anything?" Ian asked as he plopped down into the chair next to Jason. The cafeteria was fairly crowded, but there were still empty seats at other tables.

"Not much to say."

"You're not eating much."

"I guess I'm not all that hungry."

"What happened?"

"What do you mean?" Jason set down his fork. He reached for his glass and took a sip of cola. It, at least, tasted good.

"You don't seem like yourself." Ian took a bite of his sandwich. "You've changed since I saw you on Mars."

"How much can I change in three days?" Jason asked.

"You tell me...you seem different."

"I'm fine."

"Should I have one of the docs check you? The last thing the squad can afford is you—or anyone else for that matter—getting sick while we're deployed."

"I'm not sick."

"Then what the hell is your problem?" Ian kept his voice soft, so that the rest of the people in the cafeteria could not overhear him. "Why are you avoiding me?"

"I'm not—"

"Other than official duties, you've hardly poked your head out of your quarters."

"The quarters are nice." Grant's Floating Tower was a large space station, which allowed part of its structure to spin quickly enough that the rotation provided artificial gravity. "I've just been tired."

"You've been very tired since you came back from Mars. And you're still moving rather stiffly."

"It's nothing. I just pulled a muscle." *Oliver was really energetic!* "The difference in gravities is confusing me." Jason offered a shrug. "Zero gee on the *Private Reckoning*, then two-thirds gee on Mars, Earth normal up here, and now it's back to zero-gee tomorrow. Tonight. Whenever we launch. The time changes are as confusing as hell too."

Ian frowned. "You should be more adapatable then. If you plan to make a career in the BCM, then you need to be able to adapt to changing environments."

"I like being part of the security forces, don't get me wrong."

"Then you need to be able to adapt." Ian rested his hand on Jason's shoulder. "And calm down!" he said when the other man flinched.

"I will." Jason managed a smile, feeling a surge of guilt. *Ian never said we were anything more than just fuck-buddies,* he told himself. *He left me behind on Mars quickly enough.* So why did he still feel so guilty about spending the night with Oliver?

· Chapter Eight

Saturn loomed on the display monitor via a camera feed. The multi-coloured clouds swirled across its surface and its famous rings were glittering in the starlight.

Damian stared at the image. "It's quite a sight."

"Yeah, it's impressive."

Jason whistled softly. *I never thought it could look so much more amazing in person. From here, it looks like you could almost walk across the rings.* The sight made the long flight worth every last moment.

Ian pushed himself into the room, floating gently in the zero-gee. He gave them a look, then moved to bring his magnetic-soled boots into contact with the deck. His hair was in its usual spiked style. "You grunts all packed and ready?"

"Yes, Mother," Franco replied in a high-pitched voice.

Ian let the squad's laughter die away. "Good." He rested his hands on his hips. "We're not going to bother linking up with Exxon-Prime. We'll be dropping directly to the Trove colony."

"Why can't we see the station?"

"We're heading straight down into the gravity well, Damian. Orders from our corporate masters." Ian gave them all a resigned shrug. "The mission is set and you know the drill. We meet up at the shuttle bay in two hours with your basic kit. Any questions?"

"Do we need to wear our armour?"

"No, Terry, but your heavy weapons and body armour will be transported down there as cargo. Wear sidearms for the shuttle flight though. Just in case."

Franco grimaced at that.

"Any more questions?"

Jason shook his head along with the others.

"Good." Ian turned to leave. "Let's make a good impression when we land."

Well within the appointed time, Jason walked along the *Watchful Eye's* corridors from the communal bunks to the hanger bay. He moved slowly, letting his magnetically-soled boots keep his feet on the deck. The walking manner took some adjustment—each step had to bring the sole into good contact with the deckplates to ensure a solid link—but he had lots of practice at this.

The *Eye's* regular crewmen swam past him like humanoid fish. Flinging themselves through the corridors was much faster than walking.

If you've got the training and experience. Leaping about like that just makes me nauseous, Jason thought. He listened to their chatter as they moved past him, but most of it was focused on their assorted duties, using slang terms he wasn't familiar with.

A hatchway hissed open and Ian stepped through it. He was wearing his regular duty uniform and strapped on a large backpack. He had his *Mauser CG-7* PPG holstered on his thigh. "Ready for the surface and some gravity?"

"Yeah, past ready." Jason nodded. During the three week voyage out from Mars, he and Ian had not had even a single sexual encounter. *No privacy on this ship...it's worse than the* Reckoning, he thought bitterly. The *Wandering Eye* possessed a larger crew than the *Reckoning* had, and it seemed like there were always crewmen around no matter where Jason had wandered. *No chance for any personal relief action in bunks or the head.* He was getting pent-up again—he still wasn't comfortable jerking off around the others. For that matter, other than Franco, neither was anyone else. *I'm not hoping for another late night jerk-off session with Ian either.* That had been a one-time event, it seemed. *No pirate attacks to break up the monotony of the trip either. This has been one boring trip.*

"I'm looking forward to getting down there. We need some decent gravity and large corridors to run some proper simulations." Ian slapped his hand against his thigh as he walked. "A good combat drill will get us all back in shape."

Jason managed a leer. "I can think of some other *drills* we could do to get back into shape."

Startled, Ian glanced at Jason, then gave him a faint smile. "Well, we should be able to find some privacy down there. The colony is supposed to be a fairly decent size. Plenty of rooms. We're getting private quarters down there."

"Hell, right now a closet would suffice."

Ian chuckled. "You just need to work faster in the shower."

"I know, I know."

"Or be less shy. Take a lesson from Franco and—"

"No!"

"He'd be more than happy to discuss hand techniques with you."

"No, thanks."

"He's always bragging about his ability—"

"No, really. I'm not interested in having that kind of talk with him." Jason shook his head. "God!"

Ian's chuckles echoed through the corridor.

A passing crewman eyed him curiously.

Jason hoped he wasn't blushing. *I should be used to this by now.* At least his dick was behaving itself and remaining limp. *That last thing I need is to sporting wood when I walk into the hanger.*

Damian's voice drifted down the corridor. "Titan's day is the same length as its month...fifthteen Earth days."

"It's no wonder you're the computer geek," Franco replied in a resigned voice. "You're just like one. Only we can't find your off-switch."

Terry's loud laughter cut off as Ian stepped through the open door.

Jason followed Ian into the room, and then he moved closer to where Damian was standing. "How's it going?"

Damian gave him a nod. "Good."

"We're not using one of our shuttles," Terry commented. "Trove sent up one of their own. It came up from the surface."

"Really? I was under the impression that we were taking one of the *Eye's* shuttles down to Titan." Ian removed his *Transcom P2050* comp-pad from a pocket in his jumpsuit and studied the small screen. He typed a note on the keypad.

Jason stared off into space, letting his mind wander.

"The ship isn't staying here," Damian told him in a quiet voice.

"It isn't?" Jason blinked in surprise. "Where's it going?"

"It's escorting most of these freighters out to Charon."

"Out to *Charon*?" Jason shook his head. "What the hell is going on at Pluto?" The outermost planet in the solar system was a tiny icy rock. As far as he knew, there was only a tiny research outpost located there. *A punishment posting at best. Who do you piss off enough to be assigned there?* "There can't be anything of importance out there."

"There are some research facilities. Companies interested in mining for resources."

"What resources, Damian? Any mining corps would be looking at the asteroid belt or the Jovian or Saturn moons. The cost way out there would not be profitable." Jason shook his head. "It'd be a hell of a lot cheaper to ship resources in from the Orion colonies than from out past Pluto."

"Could be true. Depends on how precious the resources were. Some of the really rare transuranics might be worth it. Anyway, I heard one group is looking to use Charon as a jump-off base camp for conducting investigations of the Oort Cloud."

"How boring that would be." Franco snorted loudly. "Remind me not to sign up for *that* tour of duty."

"Come on," Ian snapped to them. He returned the pad to his pocket. "Our shuttle should be docked and waiting now." He led the squad back into the corridor and towards the hanger bay. "We're not getting paid by the hour, are we?"

"We aren't?" Brad Kellar asked. "I must have signed the wrong contract."

Jason laughed softly along with the others.

* * *

Exxon-Prime was a vast complex, floating above the orange clouds of Titan. The central core of the station was the usual ring-shaped base, rotating to generate gravity for its eighty person crew. Deployed around it, secured with just light tethers, were large tanks and cargo pods used to store the mined chemicals until freighters arrived to transport them away.

Jason stared through the porthole as the personnel shuttle maneuvered itself into low orbit. There wasn't much to see inside the shuttle after all. The passenger cabin was small and filled with seats. The cockpit was sealed off by a hatch and their pilot had not shown herself to them since she'd docked with the *Watchful Eye*.

"Look at all the freighters." Damian whistled softly as he stared through one of the portholes. "There must be fifty of them. Maybe more."

"Yeah...well, you heard Takashima. Titan has huge gas and oil reserves right?" Jason could see the cargo pods being attached to waiting freighters by spacesuited workers. "Fifty thousand pounds of cargo per pod." *Enough to fuel even Earth's insatiable demands.*

"One well-placed shot and *boom*." Franco chuckled in his deep voice. "Ka-boom."

"You like explosions just a bit too much," Joshua told him.

Franco grinned more widely.

The squad was quiet for a moment.

"How many defenders do you guys see?"

"Enough, Terry."

Jason glanced back at the structure. He couldn't actually see any of the weaponry, but he knew that Exxon-Prime mounted plasma cannons and particle beams, along with a flight of *StarWolf* fighters to fend off pirates. Given the importance and size of the fuel reserves, the Belt Consortium maintained a permanent garrison of its own, as well as providing armed escorts for the freighters.

"Is that a *Quiver*?" Damian asked suddenly and the squad turned their heads to look.

"Looks like one."

"Wow."

Jason took a second look at the angular warship. Though lightly armed, the carrier could launch forty-eight *Bolt*-class fighters into combat. It put a *Mediator* to shame. "Why the hell would a Colonial Guard carrier be out here?" he asked out loud.

"Refueling, right?" Brad shrugged.

"Makes sense to me."

Ian didn't say a word.

Jason frowned again. *The Guard have their own bases for fueling. They wouldn't rely on somewhere like Exxon-Prime unless it was an emergency.* He looked to see if he could spot any other warships—the *Quiver* should have some escorts. A *Javelin* corvette perhaps. A *Bastion*-class monitor would be a sight worth seeing upclose. The heavy monitors were the largest and most powerful warships that mankind fielded.

"I don't see anything else."

"They could be on the far side of the station," Brad said. "Or patrolling around one of the other moons. Saturn has enough of them after all."

"Space is big," Franco grumbled, "and there's only so much action to go around. You can spend a hell of a lot more time travelling to it then you spend fighting."

"Spoken like a seasoned veteren."

"Thanks."

Abruptly, the shuttle banked away from the station and dove towards the cloud-obscured surface of Titan.

"What is she doing?" Terry demanded. "We're going in too steep."

"How can you tell?" Joshua asked.

"Are you the pilot?" Damian sounded calm. "I think she know's what she's doing."

"You *hope* she does." Franco chuckled rather nastily. "I'd hate to see what kind of fireball this crate would make if we hit the ground."

"No, I think you'd like it actually." Jason managed a weak smile.

"*Get ready for some chop,*" the pilot's voice crackled over the speakers. "*It's going to be a bumpy ride down.*"

"Great," Terry muttered.

The shuttle lurched as it cut through the thickening atmosphere.

"And down we go," Joshua commented. "Express descent to hell."

"This isn't hell," Franco grumbled. "There's no enemy fire. You haven't really lived until you've made a shuttle landing while dodging missiles and particle beams. Man, that's a landing!"

"You're BCM! When have you ever made a landing under missile fire?"

Franco grinned at him. "Some of the pirates are really well-armed." Joshua groaned.

Clouds streaked past the portholes. The shuttle shuddered again.

Jason gripped the arms of his chair in a tight grip as the buffeting grew worse.

"Do you think this crate is gonna hold together?"

Jason glanced at Damian. "Why do you ask?"

"It's an old *Mark Five* model."

"So what?" Jason asked him.

"So the *Mark Fives* were always known to be a bit weak in the wings. The first production run had substandard welding."

Jason stared at him.

"You mean the freaking wings could rip off while we're flying?" There was no mistaking the irritation in Franco's voice.

"Yeah." Damian nodded his head.

"Shit."

"I can't see Yu-Wei using shuttles like that," Terry argued. "They're a huge mega-corp. They can afford top-line equipment."

"They're profitable because they cut whatever corners they can."

"Anyone see the landing pad?" Jason asked hopefully. He thought that the shaking was getting worse.

"I can't see nothing in these clouds," Terry muttered.

Ian grunted.

"Of course, I have to agree with Terry that Yu-Wei would never use such outdated equipment." Damian gave the others a quick grin. "Wouldn't be cost effective to have their shuttles crashing down all the time."

"Of course not," Franco agreed in a mocking tone. "That would be bad for the bottomline."

"And worse for us." Jason gripped the arms of his chair more tightly as the pitch of the engines changed.

"Anyway, I'm pretty sure all the *Mark Fives* were retired years ago."

The shuttle lurched and then a loud *thump* echoed through the fuselage.

"I think we're here." Ian made the announcement as a second lurch and *thump* became a prolonged shaking and shuddering.

The soft roar of the shuttle's engines faded into silence.

"We're down."

Jason opened his eyes. "Thank God for that." He glanced through the porthole.

The few surface buildings he could see were small, low-lying structures. No multi-storey towers or expansive domes here. The communications dish was probably the largest human-built object he could see.

"No other shuttles?"

"They could be kept in a hanger," Damian guessed and Joshua shrugged.

The hatchway to the cockpit hissed open. "We're down and locked," the shuttle's pilot announced. She had given herself the name Fiona Steele when she had docked with the *Watchful Eye* and taken the security team aboard. Now she gave her seven passengers a twisted smile. "You can get up now, boys. The rough part's over and done." A roughly healed scar slashed across her left cheek.

Joshua whistled softly. "She's hot."

"She's gotta be fifty!" Terry muttered back.

"She's still a looker."

Listneing to his colleagues, Jason gave her another look.

Fiona's hair was still dark, but that could be a dye job. She was fairly thin, but her face and hands did not have that sunken, aged look. Her spacesuit was an older model, worn and greasy. The drab navy blue material was covered with dozens of small patches. She wasn't wearing a helmet, but she had her suit's gloves attached to her waist.

As usual, Ian was the first man unstrapped and up on his feet. "Gear up," he ordered in a brisk tone. "Let's make all this look impressive for the locals." He took a few paces towards the shuttle's sealed main hatch, then pulled a *Transcom P2050* comp-pad out of his pocket and began to read the small display.

Jason began to unfasten his seat restraints.

A metallic *clunk* made that shuttle tremble.

Jason glanced over his shoulder, then bent down to pull a knapsack out of the storage compartment.

Damian Bowie hurried to the keypad at the airlock controls, punched in a code, and then read the tiny monitor. "We've got a good seal." The shuttle had landed on a flattened field outside of the small research complex. An umbilical tube had risen from underground to connect to the shuttle's hatch.

"Of course it's a good seal," Fiona argued. She was still standing in front of the entry to the cockpit. "I've done this a hundred times. I know exactly where to park."

"Your confidence overwhelms us," Joshua Warner replied.

Franco Morticelli just grunted as he hefted his own pack and adjusted it on his back.

Damian watched the small display flash. "There we go." The airlock beeped softly as the umbilical tube began to pressurize.

"Welcome to Titan." Fiona chuckled.

Ian didn't respond. He was still reading the screen of his comp-pad.

Joshua glanced over at Terry and they both frowned. "I hear it's a real pleasure spot."

"Yeah," Terry added. "It's a nice day to visit, ya know. It's raining out there."

"Methane rain." Damian was grinning as he stared through a small porthole next to the hatch. "We finally got assigned to a world with a real climate. I'm gonna enjoy being here. We've got real wind and rain."

"And don't forget those balmy sub-zero temperatures. Minus one fifty right?"

"Yeah," Brad agreed, "good thing I packed my flannel swim trunks."

"Stow it, guys." Ian clicked off the *Transcom P2050* and stuffed it back into his coveralls pocket. He gave his squad a final examination. "Move out."

The shuttle hatch clanked open.

"Needs a little oiling," Fiona said over the noise. "If you like whisper-quiet stuff that is. Me, I prefer to hear the gears in motion. A little grinding and stuff. Lets me know when the hatch is actually closed and not still gaping open."

Franco muttered something under his breath.

"Hope you boys don't mind walking," Fiona continued. "It's about sixty some yard to the base proper. We don't bother with tube-cars or people movers for it either. Waste of good credits."

"We can walk. No problem." Ian gave her a look. "And the cargo pods?"

"It'll all be transferred to your quarters. Should have a 'bot or two our here to get them."

"Good to hear." Ian hooked his thumb towards the hatch. "Move it out, you lot. Make it all look good for our new bosses."

"Yes,boss." Jason nodded.

Two people, a man and a woman, were waiting at end of the umbilical tube.

The man was wearing a red shirt, partially unbuttoned to show a tight gray tee-shirt underneath it, and tan slacks. He had brown hair and eyes and a sour expression on his face. He hung back, near the airlock which presumably led deeper into the main base.

The woman stepped forward. "Hello, gentlemen. I'm Claire Riley." She wore her long dark hair in an intricate series of coils and braids. "Facility administrator for Titan-Trove." Her business suit was cut in what was likely the style of the latest Earth fashions.

"Sergeant Ian Foster, newly assigned head of security." He offered her his hand and they shook. "This is my team, the Pouncers."

"I have already scanned your dossiers," Claire told him. "BCM admin forwarded the files to me within hours of your meeting with Takashima. They all seem like a competent enough team. I do not foresee any serious problems."

Head of security? Jason thought as the director continued with her welcome speech. *When did he get promoted?*

"I thought we were to back up their security?" Damian whispered to him. "Why are we suddenly taking over?"

"We're not," Franco hissed. "Ian is getting all the fancy rank. We're still just lowly grunts. He'll be a real bright-star in no time."

"Lucky us," Brad said.

"We don't need a bunch of corporate thugs showing up here." The sour-faced man finally spoke up. "Everything is under control right now. This lot will just mess things up for the rest of us."

"Mark! We've had this discussion before. Your opinion has been noted and then overruled." Claire gave her companion a sharp glare, before turning to give the security team a polite smile. "Mister Vance does not approve of the company sending in a team of outsiders to provide Trove with security."

"Not true," Mark argued. He took a step forward. "I don't approve of security in general. We don't need them."

"Yu-Wei Admin disagrees with you, Mister Vance."

"We disagree about a lot of things, Director...that's one reason why I was assigned to this backwater moon."

Jason was giving Mark a closer look. *Not too bad looking a guy,* he thought. *Not as hot as Oliver was, but still quite nice. Shame about that sour attitude though.* Abruptly, he noticed that Ian was glaring slightly. *What did I do?*

Ian looked away from Jason and then cleared his throat. "I believe that you'll find my team to be professionals. Even if we're not formally a part of Yu-Wei, we're still bound by all the usual waivers and non-disclosure agreements."

"Of course you are." Claire smiled at them.

She's smiling mostly at Ian. Jason wondered if he felt a touch of jealously at the attention she was giving him, but he was actually surprised to find that he didn't. *She smiles too much.* She seemed to have a permanent fake welcoming smile pasted on her face.

Fiona took the opportunity to limp past them. "When I get the techs to refuel the *Scrapper,* I'm gonna have a chat with Joey. There's still some vibrations coming from the spaceframe that I don't like."

"Mark Five," Damian whispered just loud enough for Jason to overhear.

"That shuttle is operating perfectly," Claire argued. "You're always complaining about something."

"I fly it. I know it." Fiona gave the director a mocking smile. "I don't tell you how to host a fundraiser...don't tell me how to fly."

Mark was smirking. "She has a point."

Claire shot him a nasty look, before turning her glare onto Fiona. "Have it your way then, *Pilot.* If you wish to squander the entire shuttle maintainence budget on meaningless tinkering, then do so."

"I will." Fiona turned and limped her way down the corridor.

Franco was smirking, but he wiped the expression from his face after Ian turned around.

Ian wore a somewhat embarrassed expresssion on own his face.

"I'll give you and your men a quick overview of the facility while we proceed to your quarters," Claire continued, turning back to Ian with a friendly smile. "Security should not be all that difficult to maintain. We're located mostly underground here. It was so much easier to take advantage of local tunnels and caverns and seal them off, rather than trying to build a full dome."

Be a hell of a lot cheaper too, Jason thought.

"The entire facility is maintained at Earth normal pressures and atmospheric mixes. Aside from the various sealed labs, of course, which have their own requirements. Trust me when I tell you to watch the signage. You would not want to venture into an isolab without a breather or a full environmental suit in some cases." Claire laughed softly. "The ambiant temperature is fairly consistent as well. "

Jason thought it was a bit cool for his taste. He was glad of his uniform's heavy weave. *I might need my jacket again,* he thought in silent amusement. He had his civvies packed into the cargo pod. *It's almost as bad as Quebecneuve.*

Ian was nodding his head in agreement. "Being underground means you just have a few limited access points."

"All of which are constantly sealed and monitored by the computer. This shuttle lock," Claire told him, "can connect with three shuttles at once." She pointed to the sealed hatches. "This inner door is military grade."

"How many external airlocks?"

"Three. One is for our vehicle bay. The other two are strictly personnel-scaled."

"Damian, I want you to check the monitor program. Make sure no one can break in without triggering alarms."

"Got it, Boss."

Ian gave Claire a friendly smile of his own. "We studied maps of this facility while outbound from Mars, but I believe that we all should have a full tour to familiarize ourselves with your facility, Director Reily."

"I would be more than happy to show *you* around, Sergeant, so that you can see exactly which sections you think you'll need to guard."

"Thank you, Director."

"Mister Vance, you can show the other soldiers to their quarters so they can unpack and settle in. You're all being quartered on sub-level two."

"Fine." Mark Vance shrugged his shoulders.

Ian shrugged out of his pack and tossed it to Franco.

"Great. I get to be your packmule again," Franco muttered.

"That's what you get for mouthing off." Ian kept his voice low. "Try being more of a team-player."

"Yeah, Sarge."

Ian sighed and rolled his eyes. "I feel like I'm babysitting children sometimes," he muttered. He turned and rejoined Claire and followed her through the airlock.

Mark stood by the open airlock for a few moments, frowning at nothing in particular, then turned to the squad. "Come on then. I don't have all day to play being tourguide."

"So what's your position here?" Terry asked.

"We keep Earth standard time here," Mark said as he stepped through the hatch and into a corridor. "The local day is fifteen days and twenty two minutes long...same as the local month."

Damian was grinning. "I already told them that."

Mark's mouth twisted into a grimace.

Jason gave Mark another look as he followed the man through the corridors. *Very nice from behind as well,* he thought. The tan slacks were on the snug side and he looked like he had a great ass. Jason licked his lips as he felt his cock twitch. *I'd like to see him in just a lab coat.*

· Chapter Nine

"We all got private bunkrooms...now just how fine is *that*?" Franco was saying with his mouth full.

Jason shook his head at Franco's manners. *He must intentionally try to be so crude,* he thought. *Though he can be amusing at times.* He popped a piece of the of orange-glazed meat into his mouth and chewed.

"Yeah, now we can sleep without listening to you beat your meat first," Joshua told Franco with a grin. Like the rest of the Belters, he was wearing the standard-issue coveralls, though being off-duty, he did not have a PPG holstered to his thigh.

"You gonna be able to sleep all by your lonesome?" Franco sneered back. "Or are you hoping for some night visits?"

Joshua flicked him the finger.

Brad guffawed loudly enough that people at the other tables looked around. Most of them seemed startled by the sound.

The Pouncers had taken over one table in the cafeteria. The walls and ceiling of that room were like the rest of the facility—cut from existing caverns and roughly finished off with cheap-looking light fixtures and exposed heating ducts. Several of the facility's regular staff were seated at various tables, eating and talking softly amongst themselves. They darted ocassional looks towards their new security guards.

"The food is good. Way better than the shit they served on the carrier." Franco stuffed another big chunk of meat into his mouth. "Even if I don't know what it is."

Damian was poking at his dinner with his fork.

"You gonna eat that or just play around with it?" Brad asked him. His own plate was already empty.

"Eat." Damian took a bite.

"I'm just gonna live in those showers," Jason announced wistfully. "Unlimited access to all that nice hot water...."

"I'll avoid them then," Franco commented.

Terry nodded agreement. "Me too."

Damian set his coffee mug back down. "Real water showers...what a fabulous luxery. I'd almost forgotten what those were like." He paused and the others nodded—with potable water at a premium, ships and space stations and most colonies limited their staff to vibe-showers. "I could stay under the spray for hours and hours." Damian sighed. "But then I get all wrinkly."

Terry shuddered. "There's a mental image I don't need."

Jason laughed along with the rest of the team. *Damian has a nice body and cute face, but he's not really my type.* He looked up as someone brushed against his back.

Ian Foster set his tray down on the table and then slid himself into an empty seat. "I don't think very much of this attempt at cornbread," he said as he took a bite of the soggy yellowish mass. "Can't they ever get the cornbread right?"

"Not bloody likely." Franco gestured with his fork. "At least the gardens are working right. The food's pretty good."

"Can you say that again, without a full mouth?" Joshua asked.

Franco gave him a grin and took even larger bites.

"Good food, decent pay, unlimited water showers...this is a dream posting." Brad Kellar leaned closer to the sargeant. "How do I get a permanent assignment here?"

Ian look at him, then shook his head.

"Nice of you to join us." Terry exchanged a look with Joshua. "We hardly see you anymore. You're always in meetings."

"It's part of my job to liase with Trove's administration."

"I bet you enjoy *liasing*," Brad murmured in a low tone. He darted a look towards Jason. "Doesn't he?"

Jason kept his expression blank.

Brad frowned.

Ian was still eating. "I can always make more time for my staff," he announced. "I can find time to amend the duty schedule and reduce your free time."

Brad flinched.

Franco snorted.

"So, Ian, what's the big secret?" Jason asked as he sipped his dark coffee. "What's the grand mystery of sub-level three?"

Ian lifted his gaze away from his own plate. He looked around, but no one else was seated close enough to overhead their conversation. "It's a research facility. Level three is mostly focused on an ongoing search for microbes." He took another bite of the meat. "If you imagine really hard, this *almost* tastes like chicken."

"It's more likely fish." Damian hunched over the table. His own plate was empty now. "There's a great big aquarium down on level three. We saw it earlier, remember?"

"Yeah, I was there."

"I was talking to one of the techs yesterday, and she told me that the aquarium is part of the water recyling system. It's also used to study fish growth in lower gravity. And for eating," Damian added brightly.

"I gathered that much."

"We're eating a science project?" Franco used his fork to spear one of the largest meat chunks still left on his plate and stared at it with a dubious expression.

"I doubt they'd feed us anything dangerous."

"You *doubt*?"

Damian shrugged. "If you don't like it, don't eat it."

"Yeah," Joshua teased. "You can also go vegetarian while you're here. Lots of stuff in the hydroponic gardens...if you're afraid to eat the meat."

Franco glanced over his shoulder. A few scientists seated at another table had stopped eating and were watching the Belters. "I'm not afraid of eating nothing." He popped the fish into his mouth and chewed it noisily.

Ian shook his head.

"There is no class to our uncouth companions," Terry announced in a fake upper class British accent.

"Indeed," Joshua agreed in a matching accent. He turned to look at Ian. "So what's the point of this place? What're they doing?"

Jason put down his fork and listened more carefully.

"From what we've seen, there's not much evidence of any serious mining going on in this area. No tunnels, no refineries. Nothing."

"No shuttle launches," Jason added. "If Trove was a serious mining operation, there should be a steady stream of shuttles heading into orbit with hydrocarbons." He paused. *And an equal stream of miners. Muscular, hunky miners pent up after long shifts out in the wilderness....*

Ian finished chewing his current mouthful, and he looked across the table at Joshua. "This is all completely confidential. If any of you so much as breath a hint of it, I will have you *spaced*. Yu-Wei is extremely protective of its corporate security."

Jason whistled softly. *Spacing* was the ulitimate punishment.

"The story about this place being used primarily to research new mining and refinery techniques is all just a cover. Claire told me that Yu-Wei is looking for evidence of life."

"Life?"

"Yeah, Terry. Life." Ian nodded. "They're hoping to find microbial lifeforms in either the sands, or else by digging deeper into the crust. There's been this theory going around since the early two thousands that life could have developed in Titan's liquid ammonia oceans."

"What kind of life is gonna live in liquid ammonia?"

"Life began on Earth in the ocean. The current theory is that something similar could be happening here." Ian shrugged. "Well, it's a big ocean over two hundred miles deep."

And that makes a difference how? Jason shook his head.

"That hardly seems like a mystery worth guarding. I can't see how it would be worth billions to other corporations or to the Colonial Guard."

Terry shrugged. "Me either, Damian."

"This is a company-funded base. It's not up to us to figure out the research programs. We're just here as guards."

"Guards for what, Sarge?" Franco grumbled. "We've seen the tour. There's nothing here to steal. No neighbours for hundreds of miles. A hostile environment beyond the airlocks. It's a waste of our time being out here."

"Yu-Wei sent us here. We're being paid good credits to walk around and look tough." Ian took a sip of his coffee. "So stop bitching."

They went back to eating.

Joshua and Terry walked back to the counter to refill their coffee cups as more of the station staff entered the cafeteria. They gave the two ladies friendly smiles and were completely ignored.

"...Tori Rhondstadt has always delivered on her promises," one of the techs was saying. She was wearing a mauve turtleneck.

Her companion had a prim expression, as if she had swallowed a lemon. "You voted for the Greens last time."

"And?"

"It didn't make much difference. EarthGov is EarthGov. Nothing ever changes."

"You're just afraid that someone is going to institute new taxes on research and development."

"It's your livelihood too."

The two Pouncers returned to their table.

"Struck out clear and plain." Franco laughed.

"You're not doing much better," Joshua told him.

"I was letting you suckers make the first move."

Terry laughed at that. "Ah, trying to make yourself look better by comparison...no doubt after he tries to make his so-called smooth play, the ladies will come flocking back to us."

Brad laughed again. "You guys just try too hard," he said. "Back home, the secret was too play 'hard to get'. Pretend you're not interested and they'd mob you."

"So how's that working for you?" Terry asked him.

"Can't you see the mobs?" Joshua countered. "We have to fight the girls off just to get back to this table."

Brad smiled, accepting their barbs. "We'll see who scores first on this base."

Jason set his empty mug down on the scuffed tabletop. "Hey, Ian, you got plans for this evening?"

"Claire invited me to a teleconference with some of the other on-moon directors. Be a good chance for me to get to know the other inhabitants of Titan."

"Oh."

"A solid working relationship with her is important to the success of our mission."

"What misson, Ian? We're isolated and from what I've seen, there's nothing worth stealing. Why not join me for a vid? You've hardly spoken to me since we left Mars."

"We were hired to do a job," Ian told him. "And that's what we're going to do. I'm sorry if our work is going to interfere with your social life."

"What the hell is that supposed to mean?"

Ian didn't reply, but he did stand up and leave the mess hall.

"Lover's quarrel?" Damian asked.

"Shut up." Jason stared at the remnants of his rapidly cooling meal. *What's up with him?* he wondered. *He can't know about Oliver. Can he? Anyway, it's not like we're engaged or something. I mean, a few handjobs back on the* Mediator *and a qucik fuck in a hotel room? We're not even dating.*

Jason stood up and left his tray on the table.

* * *

Currently alone, Jason walked through Trove's uppermost level. He was wearing his crimson and brown coveralls, along with his pistol, but no body armour or heavy weapons. *No need to wear everything unless we actually have a crisis situation to deal with.* He agreed completely with Ian's decision. *We'd look ridiculous wandering around in all that crap.*

He was taking the chance to wander around on his own, getting a feel for the place and seeing what he could learn on his own after the quick tour Mark had given them. Two days on-station was not really long enough to memorize the layout.

The base seemed fairly secure. Trove was located in a fairly obscure location on Titan, the bulk of the facility was mostly underground which minimized the chances of it being spotted by orbiting spacecraft, and access to the surface was limited.

Still, only having seven security guards hardly seems sufficient if someone did try and take over. Trove had a staff of fifty or so. Thirty of them were researchers and scientists, and the rest were admin and techs. *Ian is still trying to find out who has combat training in case of emergencies.*

Jason had a better question for him. *Where was the* regular *security team? Surely Yu-Wei kept some of its own personnel here.* But where were they now? *They can't be entirely reliant on the techs and researchers picking up weapons to defend themselves, can they? Or does Trove have something more exotic with which to defend itself?* What was the lab actually researching?

"More questions than answers," he muttered to himself as he continued walking.

The corridors of the facility were more like tunnels than proper hallways. Mark had explained that they had been bored out of Titan's rocky surface and roughly sealed by a high temperature plasma field—a feature of the *Mole Machines* used to dig the tunnels—finished in some places, and then strung with lights and ducting for the life support system.

"Basic, low-cost, quick construction." Jason was not surprised really—every single company liked to keep a tight watch on the bottom line after all.

Sub-level one was the first main base floor—twenty, maybe thirty feet underground—and pretty much deserted. The vehicle garage, containing a few dust buggies and rovers, took up most of the space, with some storage rooms, and a small computer bay.

"Deserted unless someone is conducting maintenance in the garage or getting ready to go outside." Jason stopped in front of an open hatch and looked through. *Or not, it seems.* "Mind if I join you?"

"Make yourself at home," Mark replied in a rather sour tone from where he was sitting at a console. "My opinion doesn't matter to anyone in authority anyway."

"Don't be like that," Jason told him as he stepped into the tiny control centre. "It wasn't our choice to come here either, you know. Company orders."

Mark didn't reply.

One of the consoles beeped softly.

Jason took a long look around the room. It was maybe ten square feet in size, cramped with computers and displays. Most of the consoles were blinking and flashing. "So you get to look after the control room?"

"Hardly. This is just traffic control. Main Ops is back down on level two."

I knew that, Jason thought. "Yeah, you gave us had the basic tour." *And now we have some free time to wander around the unrestricted areas. Get ourselves familiar with the terrain.* He wasn't really interested in the mess hall, lounge, or gymnasium on level two, and the labs and research facilities on level three were still off-limits to the Pouncers. "I just thought I'd come up here and look around a bit."

"Look all you want." Mark waved his hand towards a display. "I get to sit here all day and watch traffic pass by. Two dozen heavy bulk shuttles a day launching into orbit to deliver fuel to Exxon-Prime...and just as many coming back down to land and reload at their home ports."

"Sounds exciting."

Mark snorted loudly. "Shaw, you were the first shuttle to land *here* in four months. For all that Fiona boasts, she's not done more than tinker on the *Scrapper* in all that time."

Wow, we are *more isolated than I thought.* "Call me Jason."

Mark was staring at the monitors and did not reply.

Jason took advantage of that to let himself eye the other man. *The lines in his face give him some character—he's aging with that rugged look.* "Surely you have other duties here than just sitting around staring at monitors. I mean, a computer program could do that."

"It's my job...with the computer for back-up when I'm busy." Mark shook his head. "I can do this down in Ops, but I like the solitude. No one comes up here. Usually." He reached out to tap a button. "I'm a back-up shuttle pilot as well."

"Now that sounds important."

"Just left-over from Colonial Guard training."

"You were in the Guard?"

"Just one tour." Mark shrugged. "The usual post-high school tour. Earn some extra money for college and fulfil my patriotic duty." He snorted again. "The worst decision I ever made. Short of taking the assignment to come and work here that is."

"Is that where you learned to pilot?"

"Yeah."

Jason pretended to a study a display showing a crawler slowly leaving the garage lock, while in reality he was making a closer study of

Mark. *It looks like he's got a nice body. His face is pretty—when he's not frowning.* He didn't have the typical square-jaw hero look, but he was still pretty hunky. *What are the odds that he'd be interested in having some fun with me?* Jason wondered. *Probably not all that great. Better not risk it.* Isolated postings were just as bad as being aboard a ship when a romance went bad.

And it's pretty obvious how well that fling with Ian worked out. Gonna make the tour rather tense. When they returned to Mars, he'd have to apply for a transfer to some other squad. *Ian will probably approve it quickly enough. Next time I am not jumping a team-mate. No way.*

He sat down in a spare chair. *Can't stop me from fantasizing though.* Trove had a distinct advantage over the ships on which he'd been serving. *Plenty of private space for a man to get himself off.* Jason realized that he was sporting a hard-on, tenting out the front of his coveralls. *Did he notice?* Luckily, Mark wasn't looking at him and hadn't noticed. *Yeah, Mark's a hunk. I wonder what he looks like without his shirt?*

Finally Mark looked up, almost startled to see that Jason was still in the room. "You want a coffee or something?"

"Sure."

Mark stood up. "I gotta go take a leak anyway. I'll be right back."

Jason admired the sight of just how well Mark's slacks fit his tight butt. *This assignment could have some extra benefits after all,* he thought happily. *As long as I don't push things, of course. Ian would shoot me if I screwed up our relations with the locals.*

Not that the sergeant would likely notice. He was pretty much occupied with daily meetings with Claire Riley.

Whatever we might have had is over...Ian's not interested in me. Admitting that hurt a bit. *Either I was just a shipboard fling or else I lost him after Mars.* Jason couldn't tell what had happened. Was he looking for something more, or just a fling? *What do I want?* he wondered. *Besides a few minutes in the showers with Mark....*

· **Chapter Ten**

Jason shrugged off the chest-plate of *his KR-8/BX* hostile environment armour. "I'm sweating like a horse under all this crap." The outer suit was composed of fifteen pieces of armour plating; each segment could be removed independently of the rest, while providing twelve hours of oxygen. The undersuit was designed to keep the wearer warm. "I think the temperature controls are acting up."

Ian cleared his throat. His normally spiked hair-style was flattened from having been under his helmet. "The patrols are necessary. You all know that." He had been running the Pouncers from one end of the facility to the other while wearing full armour. "We need to be familiar with Trove's layout in case of attack."

Terry shook his head. "Who the hell is going to attack us? The microbes or the sand?" He was holding his helmet in his hand. His own hair was sweat-dampened.

"Yeah," Damian said as he stuffed his own helmet back into his locker. "Think about it. To get to us, you'd have to breach one of the airlocks first and the alarms would sound. The locks are solid...no one is going to break in that way."

"Someone could tunnel their way in."

"Not bloody likely." Franco laughed. "We'd hear them for sure! *Mole Machines* or explosives, it won't be quiet."

"But it is certainly possible."

"I'm not so sure that anyone else is likely to try that," Jason replied. "I think the company is overreacting."

Ian shrugged in response. "Wouldn't be the first time some head office got worked up over its field branch. Not our concern either. It's our job to remain ready for anything."

"We're not Colonial Guard marines you know."

"Yeah, we're Belter Militia."

"So we're already better than the Colonial Guard." Ian hooked his thumb towards the lockers. "Finish stowing your gear and then go get cleaned up. Joshua and Franco, you two lucky guys get to join me for a sweep around the surface."

"Why us?"

"Because I said so. We'll take airlock two, I think."

Jason unzipped his crimson coveralls a few inches, trying to cool himself down. *Why the hell does he make us run around like this?* he wondered. *Full armour is bad enough, but then to have wearing these big packs? Added weight training be damned...that man just likes to make us all miserable.* It was part of the training routine though, and although the team grumbled, everyone listened. *I suppose we might be called on to run a mile while carrying someone's unconscious body.* He hoped not though. *It better be someone light.*

Ian picked up his helmet. "The rest of you get to take the external tour with me tomorrow."

"Oh joy," Terry said.

"So let's get to it." Ian gestured towards Franco and Joshua. "Suit yourselves back up...it's gonna be chilly out there."

Leaving the others, Jason paced down the rough corridor towards his quarters—each of the privates rooms boasted its own small but functional bathroom. The security team had been assigned to rooms set along a corridor just outside of the main living area. *Together, yet isolated from the rest of the locals. Typical. Course, the way I smell right now, it's probably for the best.* "God, I need a shower."

"That's one good thing about the colony. We've got a decent shower."

Jason froze in mid-step.

"Sorry, I startled you."

"No, Mark, it's fine. I just didn't see you there."

The company man shrugged. "I'm used to it." He was leaning against the rough stone wall with his arms crossed in front of his chest.

He was wearing a baggy blue tee-shirt and loose fitting black cargo-style pants.

"Sorry, just got done a real long patrol and I was thinking about how nice a shower would feel. Christ, I forgot about that aspect! You guys have *real* water showers here...not just those damned vibe things."

"Yes, we have a *real* water shower."

"I envy you!" Jason told him. "I hate vibers." With water at such a premium onboard ships and most installations, vibe-showers were generally used. A one-minute mixture of sonic waves and anti-bacterial lighting was hygienic enough, but hardly as satisfying as having one's body pounded by a real shower. *Our quarters have vibe-showers, but the communal showers near the gym are water ones.*

"There's plenty of water around here."

"I keep forgetting about that." Titan was mostly composed of water ice and rock so it was a simple and even cheap matter for potable water to be obtained. *I value unlimited water showers as being so much more valuable than all the hydrocarbons around here.* "Lucky lucky me." Jason looked towards the showers, then back at Mark. *Do you want to come along and wash my back?* he thought about asking.

Mark turned down another of the corridors and quickly vanished.

With a sigh, Jason turned and headed towards the gym facility. *Well,* he thought, *I am already all sweaty. Maybe I should check out the gym again.*

As he trudged his way towards the gym, he allowed himself a little harmless mental indulgence about some of the staffers he had seen. *There must be a good fifty people here at least.* The tunnels and caverns stretched out a considerable distance. *There's no way I've seen everyone yet.*

There was one particular tech he had seen earlier, welding something on one of the crawlers in the garage. His name tag had read *Corwin.*

Jason stepped through the hatch into the gym. There were treadmills and some weight lifting machines and a few devices he couldn't name. He looked around again. *This place is seriously well-equipped. Yu-Wei spent some major credits here.*

"Everything you need to keep yourself in shape."

Jason twisted his head to the right. "Hi." He felt his knees tremble slightly. *It's my cute tech!*

"Hi. I'm Ted." The blond man offered his hand. "Ted Corwin. I know you're part of the new security detail, but I didn't catch your name on the memo."

"Jason Shaw." He tried not to stare, but given that Ted was only wearing a really loose tee-shirt and tight shorts, it was hard not too. He finally let go of the man's hand.

"Welcome to Titan. It's always nice to see new faces." Ted looked to be in his early twenties. "We got bored rather easily."

"I can imagine. I'm used to ship duty...the same faces and very limited space for weeks on end." Jason hooked his thumb at the size of the room they were standing in. "This room alone has more open space than the last ship I was on."

"Space isn't at any premium around here," Ted told him. "Easy enough to tunnel out whatever we need. The first crews got a bit carried away actually. There were a lot more sections built here than we ended up needing." He shrugged. "Apparently the company changed its mind about the size of the staff to be assigned here."

"Odd that they'd waste the money on building it all first though." Jason offered his own shrug. "Most corporations pinch every credit."

"Tell me about it." Ted gestured. "You here to work out, or just looking?"

"I plan to work out."

"Good. I like having company."

"Me too." Jason headed over to the tiny locker room to change. He was slightly excited at the thought of being alone with this hunk, but he quickly reminded himself about the potential consequences of making an unwanted advance. *Ian would probably shoot me. Claire would certainly want me transferred out.* He didn't need a black mark on his record. *Things are strained enough with Ian right now...* And then there was Mark. *No, there isn't any* Mark.

Jason unzipped his coveralls and hung them on a hanger. Dressed in just his snug boxer-style shorts and a tight gray tee-shirt, he headed back to the weight room and found Ted already pressing weights.

Ted was shirtless now, and his pair of skin-tight shorts left absolutely nothing to the imagination. He had a thick coat of blond hair on his chest to match the hair on his head.

Jason watched the muscles stretch and strain and he licked his lips. Then he realized that he was being pretty blatant in staring, so he started working out.

Ted chuckled softly.

Jason glanced back towards him. *Is he checking me out?* It looked like Ted was sneaking glances at him.

"It sure looks like neither you nor I need to worry about freezing if the life support gives out," Ted finally commented.

Jason glanced down at his own hairy chest. "Yep, guess not."

Ted was smiling as he continued to work out.

After a little while, Ted told Jason that he'd had enough weights for tonight. "I think I'll take a quick shower and then head for the steam room."

Jason kept lifting weights, but all the while he was thinking about this stud in the steam room. *I do love steam rooms.* He found them to be such sensual places—as the steam enveloped him and made his skin tingly. *It gets me all worked up.*

Pretty soon, he was sporting a serious erection in his shorts. He decided that it was time to head for the showers. *Before someone walks in on me. I'm not sure I'd care to try and explain this to anyone.* He undressed at his locker, yanking off his tee-shirt and boxer shorts and letting his hard-on spring free. Jason hurried into the shower cubicle.

Ted was still in there, standing under one of the heads. His skin was red with the heat and steam.

Jason's earlier hard-on had finally started to go down, but once he noticed that Ted had a semi-erection, he started to harden again. *We both have nice cocks,* he noticed. Ted had a large plum-shaped head, and his low-hanging balls were dusted with hair.

Ted smiled at him, looking at Jason's erection with open admiration and desire. "'Bout time you showed up. Come on in here with me." He turned and headed back to the steam room.

"Ah, what the hell?" After some thought, Jason decided to join him.

He opened the door and was engulfed in a thick cloud of steam. It took his eyes a few moments to adjust to the dim light, but he quickly spotted Ted's shadow as he stood leaning against the far wall. Jason walked in farther and sat down on one of the benches. "Nice place."

"We like to think so."

Jason had a hard time talking in the heat and he was far too interested in snatching quick looks at Ted's crotch. Ted's cock was semi-erect and all of a sudden it twitched and started rising.

Jason stood up and looked straight at Ted.

Ted was grinning back at him.

When their eyes met, Jason's cock also started twitching. Within moments, both of them were fully hard, their cocks pointing at each other.

"So, do you like what you see?" Ted took a step closer to Jason and their cock-heads touched lightly. Both men flinched slightly, but kept staring into each other's eyes and the lust and excitement was almost unbearable.

"Yeah, I do." Jason reached out and lightly touched Ted's nipples. *Rock hard,* he thought as his hands massaged the other man's pecs.

Ted reached his arm behind Jason's back and pulled him closer. "I don't get a lot of company in the sauna," he said in a soft tone of voice as they embraced.

Jason moaned softly as he felt both of their cocks gliding together between their bellies. He kept his fingers brushing across Ted's nipples, making the other man moan out with pleasure.

Ted pulled Jason in closer and as their hips collided, it sent shockwaves right down to their toes. Both of their cocks were leaking pre-cum and it mixed in their body hair creating a lubricated passageway for their cocks to slide around in. Ted's hands were playing with Jason's ass cheeks pulling him in and out creating a friction between their stomachs. Then Ted brought his mouth to Jason's and they kissed, their tongues quickly duelling between their hot mouths. Jason's hands held Ted's head and they kept kissing as their bodies were dancing together, cocks sliding wetly together.

Ted then started kissing Jason's neck, then his chest, and then his tongue sank lower and lower to finally lick the tip of Jason's cock.

Jason let out a loud moan as Ted took his shaft into his mouth and started sucking on it. "Fuck, that feels good." Jason guided Ted slowly to a bench—the other man never letting go of his cock—and as Ted lay down Jason bent over to take in Ted's cock into his wet mouth.

Both men were pumping their cocks into each other's mouth and their cocks were now rock hard. Ted let go of Jason's cock to start liking and sucking at his balls. They were both growling and moaning quite loudly and the sounds added to the sexual tension bringing them closer to the brink.

Jason stood up and turning his body around lay down next to Ted as their mouths found each other again and their tongues shared the tastes of pre-cum. They ground their hard-ons together.

Ted took both cocks into his hand and both men pumped their cocks together, their balls slapping against each other.

"Oh, fuck yeah!" Ted gasped as they erupted at the same time sending load after load of hot cum splashing across their bellies.

Jason slumped back, gasping for breath in the hot steamy air. "Wow," he said. "Just wow."

"Fuck, that was great," Ted commented, equally winded. "You've obviously had some practice at that."

"Well, yeah."

"Good to know...not enough skilled cocksuckers around here." Ted laughed.

Jason wiped his forehead.

"I usually use the gym and sauna every other night around this time..." Ted gave him a smile. "It's almost always deserted."

"I'll have to keep that in mind." Jason looked down at himself. "I'm all sticky."

"And really really sweaty." Ted cracked the door open and looked outside. "It's clear. Come on...join me in the shower?"

"You bet." Jason eagerly followed him back across to the shower cubicles, hoping for round two.

* * *

"So what's over in the other section?"

Ian frowned and looked up from the *Transcom P2050* comp-pad he had been reading from. "What other section?" Aside from the Belters, the lounge was empty. It was a fair-sized room, with eight chairs for each of the two tables, a wall-mounted computer screen, and a small alcove holding a basic assortment of snacks and drinks.

Joshua punched his shoulder. "Don't play dumb with us."

"Yeah," Damian added. "There's a whole other section of this complex, built off level two, and it's not showing up on any of our maps." He waved his own comp-pad. "I thought you were big on us having full access to this place in case of invasion or attack."

"Yeah," Franco grunted. "So spill it." He had a light bristling of hair on his head and had been muttering earlier about needing to shave it again.

Terry tossed a few credit-chips into the centre of the table and dealt himself another card from the deck as Brad, Franco, and Damian watched.

Ian shrugged. "Claire said it was just a rough cavern. Some tunnels were excavated through the rocks during the initial construction. Before Trove's layout was finalized, I guess. There's no important facilities there."

"So why was it built?" Joshua returned to the table and the card game with a fresh drink in his hand.

"Better question." Jason cleared his throat. "Why is access to it locked off?"

Ian looked at him blankly.

"Locked and coded." Damian nodded his agreement with Jason. "Triple encrypted too. The access codes to the airlocks or the shuttle umbilicals are child's play compared to this one."

Ian's eyes widened. "You've been trying to hack into the mainframe?"

Damian nodded his head. "You told me to check into security, Sarge. I was just following your orders." He paused, watching as Ian closed his eyes and slowly shook his head. "There's a power flow to it and some hardwired computer links too. I can't call up the duty roster, but several researchers here in Trove are listed as *duty unassigned*. I'd guess that they've been assigned there."

Ian frowned.

"It's part of our job to be prepared. I'd hardly call us prepared if there's an entire section blocked off from us."

"You might be right, Corporal." Ian spoke formally. "I'll have to talk with Claire about this little oversight."

Jason shook his head. *Oversight? She deliberately hid this from you. From all of us. I want to know why.*

"I'll definitely have a talk with her," Ian continued.

"The *Cradle* is a restricted area." Mark stepped around the corner of the corridor and into the small lounge. "Off-limits to pretty much everyone."

"I don't think any place should be off-limits to me," Ian told him. "I *am* the head of security around here."

"For now."

Ian's face darkened at both his words and his tone. "Listen up, Mister Vance. I'm the authorized head of security—"

"Until the company decides otherwise."

Franco laughed loudly. "I like him," he announced, giving Mark a friendly smile. "He treats you with the same attitude the rest of us do."

Ian grimaced. "Shut up, Franco." He slipped his *Transcom P2050* back into one of the pockets on his coveralls. "I guess I'll just have to have a word with Director Riley about this lapse."

"I suppose that you will." Mark nodded.

Without another word, Ian hurried out of the lounge.

Mark watched him go.

Jason watched Mark. *Are you just trying to stir up trouble?* he wondered. *Helping us solve a mystery, or just trying to turn Claire against us?*

"Care to join us?" Joshua was shuffling cards. "We've always got room for another hand at this game. What's it called again?"

"Draco Poker." Franco reached for a set of dice and eyed them rather dubiously. "It's like regular poker, only you roll these dice every so often and the cards change values based on what gets rolled."

"I was winning until that last roll made the emperor of stars worthless." Damian frowned at the cards in his hand. "At least I think I was. It's harder to keep track of the cards when you have seven different suits."

"And the dice."

"Well yeah," Damian nodded towards Terry. "And the dice."

"I've got better ways to spend my money than waste it gambling." Mark turned on his heel and strode away.

Jason watched Mark wander back down the corridor. *He does look very nice from behind,* he thought. His butt fills out those slacks really nicely.

"You're drooling," Damian said in a soft voice.

"No, I'm not."

"Yeah, you are. But don't worry...I won't tell."

"Shut up." Jason walked towards the small refreshment alcove.

· Chapter Eleven

"The Cradle is a restricted area, Sergeant Foster." Claire Riley managed to keep her tone civil, though her narrowed eyes showed some strain. "I'm not sure how you found out about it, but when I find the leak, the punishment for that person will be severe."

"How and why doesn't matter," Ian told her in an equally civil tone. "Anyway, that revelation would fall under the heading of 'a security breach' which would then make it my responsibility to investigate and punish."

Claire blinked at him in surprise.

Jason Shaw was frowning too. The corridor seemed like an odd location to host a meeting, but that was where Ian had called Claire to meet him. She had arrived several minutes late, and seemed taken back when she realized that Ian had brought his entire squad along with him.

"I've heard that the Cradle doesn't contain any important facilities," Ian continued, not giving her a chance to recover. "It's a secondary facility, compared to this main part. At least, that's what the one accessible file I found said."

Ian was standing and staring at the sealed hatchway. That particular corridor struck out away from Trove, passed by two storage lockers and then just stopped at a bulkhead. "It's just a separate laboratory, isn't it?" The hatch was locked and his universal pass-code had been denied. "A lab built over a mile away from the rest of the complex."

Claire Riley glanced at the squad of soldiers standing close by—looking so militant in their uniforms and carrying pistols and other gear as if ready for a fight—and then she smiled tightly. "Closer to two miles actually. A security precaution. For maximum containment in the event of anything...*unforeseen*."

Jason frowned. *What type of dangerous experiments are you running? Are we in danger of getting ourselves killed?*

"I think I should go and check this Cradle out."

"The company might have assigned you to be in charge of security for *this* facility, despite my better judgement, Sergeant Foster, but that hardly gives you a high enough clearance to see *everything* being done here. Many of the experiments are exceedingly sensitive. All of them are classified."

"I'm no scientist, Director. Simply looking at an experiment in progress is not going to reveal any of your deep dark secrets to me."

She grimaced. "I would not be so certain of that."

"I insist." Ian kept his voice polite, though it was more strained than usual. He was resting his hand on his holstered pistol. "I was given full clearance to oversee Trove's security. That was the deal—I have that confirmation in my records. This tunnel was never mentioned to me...it could pose a potential threat."

Claire laughed lightly. "The Cradle is probably the most secure location Trove has," she told him.

"I'd still like to be the judge of that."

Claire sighed loudly. "The tunnel has five separate bulkheads...each of which has a military grade rating. Warship grade armour. It would take a nuclear blast to breach one."

Ian frowned at her. "Multiple bulkheads to safeguard the tunnel to one minor lab?"

"It's a very sensitive location," she reminded him. "I would be lying if I said that it was not the most important and valuable location on Titan."

"All the more reason that I check on its security."

"Have it your way then. Fiona is making a shuttle run out there shortly."

"Shuttle?" Ian was obviously confused by her sudden change of heart.

Jason and the other Pouncers exchanged equally confused looks.

"Why go by shuttle if you have this underground tunnel?" Franco demanded.

"The Cradle has a small dome built overtop of it. Environmental monitoring is the cover story Yu-Wei has circulated among the other inhabitants. Fiona ferries out some of the larger equipment and bulk supplies to the staff there periodically—to help maintain the illusion. Small things are taken via the tunnel."

"So there is a potential breach."

"Hardly, Sergeant. I cannot see anyone breaching that dome. No one else on Titan, or even off-world, knows that the Cradle even exists."

"Not even MWX?"

Claire's casual smile faltered. "They scarcely bother ever leaving their digs on Mars. I do not believe they have any interest in Saturn and its moons."

Ian gave her a smile. "One of the reasons given to me for our assignment here, Director, was because of a new MWX team being assigned to Titan. Vice-Pres Takashima was quite alarmed by the simple possibility of their presence. I would've thought that they would be an equal concern of yours?"

"Well they are not. Whatever Multi-World Expeditions chooses to do with its researchers is hardly a concern of mine."

"As you say, Director."

Claire sniffed. "I will inform Fiona to expect a few passengers. The shuttle doesn't have enough space to carry your entire squad. It will be carrying important cargo, after all."

"Of course," Ian agreed. "I'll only take one of my men with me."

Claire turned away. "Good day then." She hurried off along the corridor, back towards the main portion of the base.

"Brad, you're going with me. Squad dismissed," Ian told them. "Go back to your quarters and continue your daily routine."

As the squad walked along the tunnel, Damian appeared lost in thought.

"Earth to Damian." Jason tapped him on the shoulder. "Are you there?"

"Huh?" Damian blinked, then gave his head a shake. "What were you saying?"

Jason shook his head. "I was wondering what planet you're currently on. You tuned us all out." The rest of the squad had left the pair of them behind.

"I was just wondering why Multi-World Expeditions would be setting up a base here." Damian's fingers were idly tapping against the *Transcom P2050* clipped to his waist. "They tend to focus their efforts on dead worlds where they can dig through the ruins of alien civilizations."

"Graverobbing whatever they can find," Mark Vance said as he fell into step with them. His shirt and pants were rumpled and stained with what looked like grease. He looked tired, with bags under his eyes.

"*Scavenging* is a more accurate term," Damian told him.

Mark snorted loudly.

Jason shook his head, this time in slow resignation. *Mark does like to argue with everyone!* he thought. Mark's shirt was partially unbuttoned, offering tantalising hints at how his chest looked.

"They're just a bunch of government-approved tombrobbers!" Mark snarled. "I've seen a few of their camps. They squat in the ruins and dig up anything which might be even remotely valuable. They're certainly not archelogoists. They're not much better than bandits."

"It's not pretty, or nice," Damian agreed, "but it *is* important. I mean, we're pretty primitive compared to most of the aliens. We need to advance our technology somehow."

"Or else risk being conquered?"

"That trio of Draco survey ships which stumbled across the Solar System could have outgunned and outfought the entire existing Guard at the time. Those three ships were just lightly armed exploration vessels....glorified freighters. A single Draco battle cruiser could have vaporized every warship Earth possessed."

Jason nodded his agreement. *We were lucky the Dracos weren't looking for a military conquest. We'd never have stood a chance.*

"And now we can defend ourselves?" Mark challenged.

"In eighty years, we still haven't really advanced all that much," Damian told him honestly. "Yeah, the Dracos sold us FTL propulsion, and a few other pieces of technology, for a decent profit. They let us venture out into the galaxy and establish coloines, amused themselves by watching us stumble through meeting other aliens.

"Oh, we can put up more of a fight now. We can make an alien conquest a lot more costly, but I don't buy into most of the propaganda the Guard publish."

Jason shook his head again. They kept walking.

"The Guard are still not much more than a jumped-up police force."

Mark's mouth hung open.

"Sure, they're getting better equipped," Damian continued, "but they're still not up to the standards of the other races. If a war started, I doubt we'd last very long."

"And what about you Belters?"

"Oh, we're just glorified police and customs agents. The old Earth term would have probably been *Coast Guard*. If the Sol System was invaded, we'd fight back but we'd get slaughtered right along with the Guard."

Mark glanced towards Jason, then looked back at Damian. "You are a such a database of trivia."

"It's a gift."

"The way I see it," Jason interrupted, "is that the Terran Colonial Union either needs to make itself too costly to conquer, or else not be worth the effort."

"Exactly." Mark nodded. "So what's the solution? Confine ourselves to one world, be too primitive to bother with? Or expand and colonize as many worlds as possible to make ourselves too big and powerful to attack?"

"I prefer the latter," Jason told him. "We've made ourselves known to the galaxy. We can't hide away again."

"The Dracos know about us. So the Takakas. The Suimmas, the Brokora...we've got a few trade partners."

"Other than the Dracos, the others are minor powers."

"They're the best kind to deal with," Mark told him. "Not a big risk. The TCU is their equal in size and power."

Maybe not in military power, Jason thought. "The Takakas think that we're worth the effort of conquering. They've got ships prowling around our borders."

"So, we need to make a treaty." Mark stopped walking and turned to glare at the other two men. "Going to war over Epsilon Indi isn't worth it."

"Not defending our colonies will send the wrong message."

"Why do you say that, Jason?" Mark looked at him.

Jason looked right back. "Because it would tell the other aliens that we're weak. It would be an open invitation for them to invade the Union."

"And if we go to war and lose? That would definitely show those other races that we're weak."

"Well, yeah, but surely—"

Mark laughed loudly. "Damned if we do, and damned if we don't?"

"Pretty much," Jason agreed.

Damian shook his head and sighed.

* * *

Fiona was standing near the umbilical-tube which led to the shuttle when Ian Foster walked through the airlock, with Brad Kellar and Jason Shaw in tow.

"Morning lads." Fiona smiled at them both. She was wearing her usual worn and heavily patched flightsuit, with her helmet clipped to her belt. "You're early. We're still getting the cargo loaded."

Ian was wearing his usual uniform coveralls, with light body armour strapped overtop the fabric, and his pistol on his hip. He was obviously setting out to make an impression on anyone working in the Cradle. "Are we taking your shuttle?"

"No, I thought we'd walk there."

Mark stepped back through the umbilical and stopped to watch. He was dressed in a grease-stained flightsuit. He glanced at the security guards, his eyes lingering on Jason for a moment longer than on the others, then he looked at Fionna.

Jason eyed him back. *He looks good in everything he wears,* he thought.

"A two mile jaunt will do us all some good." Ian looked at the pilot, matching her cocky grin. "Assuming, of course, that *you* are up to it?"

"Course I am, lad." She thumped her right fist against her legs—they made a solid metallic *thunk.* "These things are still solid. I've got another two years before the warranty fails."

Ian let his mouth hang open for a moment.

Mark shook his head. "Are you quite finished?" he asked.

"Yeah, for now." Fiona gave him a wink, then she turned to leer at Ian. "But once I get soldier-boy here alone in the cockpit, then all bets are off."

Ian rolled his eyes.

"Better you than me...Sir." Brad chuckled softly.

Ian glared back at him.

"Be careful, Fiona." Mark's voice held a note of concern.

"I'm always careful," she replied. There was a faint smile on her face as she patted his shoulder. "Gonna be a milk run. Like it always is." She chuckled. "Still, flight-time is flight-time and that's always enjoyable."

Ian looked at his watch, then at her. "When do we leave?"

"A few more minutes. Right, Mark?"

"Yep." He nodded, then turned his head to look down the corridor. "I'll just check on the last few cargo pods."

"Make sure they're strapped in right this time. I don't want them shifting around on me during the flight."

"I know the drill."

"You do, but I'm not sure about those new labourers. I think Claire's looking to save credits by hiring idiots."

"Fiona!"

"You know what I mean. Brawn for the labour, not brains. If you can sign your name on the forms, then you're probably overqualified." She gave Ian and Brad a grin. "A lot like soldier-boys, I dare say." She paused. "I thought it was just two of you?"

"Corporal Shaw is staying here," Ian told her.

"Good...I made the calculations based on weight. Having another body onboard would make my math wrong."

"I'm not going," Jason said. "I like my feet firmly on the ground."

* * *

Jason walked across the cafeteria with his tray and stopped by one of the tables. "Morning, Ted."

"Morning, Jason." Ted rubbed at his eyes, then blinked repeatedly. "Morning comes way too early for me. Can't we adopt a longer day? Or start the day at eleven?"

"Now that's an idea." Jason smiled down at the other man. "I feel the same way." He remained standing, holding a tray in his hand. "I've never been good at getting up while it's still dark outside."

"And you work onboard spaceships? Damn, you are a glutton for punishment."

"Well...."

Ted managed a tired chuckle. "Yeah, you're a glutton for other things too."

Grinning in agreement, Jason gave the cafeteria a quick scan, checking out the few other people present. He didn't see any of the other Pouncers. *Some of them should be on break. Wonder where they are?*

Mark Vance was seated at a table by himself. He had a comp-pad in his hand, and was idly reading its screen. He had changed out of his flightsuit for a loose tee-shirt and jeans.

"He looks lonely."

Ted yawned, then stood up. "I need more coffee," he muttered. "Way too early in the morning for me. I gotta get moving for my shift." He poked Jason in the arm. "Forget about him. Vance likes his privacy. Stuck up prick," he muttered barely loud enough to be overheard. "I think Fiona is the only person he ever bothers being talking too. Except to argue...he'll argue with anyone."

"I see." Jason watched Ted stumble towards the coffee machine, then he sauntered across the floor towards Mark's table. "Can I join you?" he asked.

Mark looked up from the comp-pad and shrugged. "Don't care." A half-eaten bagel was on his plate, but his coffee mug was empty.

Jason sat down. The mess hall was barely a quarter full, but he knew which table he wanted to sit at. *Seeing as Ted had to leave for his shift, that just leaves one hot guy for me to check out.* "Anything interesting on the agenda for today?" He took a sip of his coffee. There was a small tuft of dark chest hair showing above the collar of Mark's tee-shirt.

Mark shook his head and chuckled ruefully. "Not around here. This is one of the most uninteresting locations on Titan. If you wanted excitement, you should have gotten yourself assigned to one of the refineries. At least they have daily shuttle launchings and stuff."

"Maybe I like peace and quiet."

"And mind-numbing boredom?"

"That's why the company pays us the big bucks, right?"

Mark snorted loudly. He reached for his pad again.

Jason set his fork down. The scrambled eggs were powdery. *I hate instant eggs,* he thought in distaste. *When will I learn to stop ordering them while at these posts?* You just couldn't get decent eggs off-Earth. *Unless you're a rich exec willing to pay ten credits an egg.* The bacon wasn't bad though—it could be shipped frozen after all.

"I thought you'd have gone with your buddy."

"To the Cradle?" Jason shrugged. "My name didn't come up in the roster."

"He took Brad with him." Mark was staring intently at Jason. "I think Fiona had her eyes on him too."

"Ian's a popular guy." Jason took a sip of his coffee. He tried to keep his tone light. "Everyone likes him."

There was a sudden rumbling and the mess hall went quiet.

Jason almost dropped his mug as his chair swayed and nearly fell over. He kept his grip on both mug and chair, though coffee slopped across the table. "Earthquake?" he asked in alarm.

A glass rolled off the table and shattered on the floor.

Breathing heavily, Jason noticed that the rest of the cafeteria's occupants didn't appear to be panicking—they were still sitting and talking calmly. A few were glancing around idly.

"What gives?" he demanded as the tremor ended as quickly as it had started. "No one mentioned earthquakes in the briefing."

"Wasn't an earthquake." Mark shook his head. "*Titanquake* is the correct term. But that was most likely just a cryovolcano erupting." At Jason's puzzled expression, he smiled. "Didn't you read the briefings?"

"Sure I did. But none of them mentioned quakes."

"Well Titan's surface is composed of layers of ice and rocks, and they're all riding on an ocean of liquid ammonium sulfate. The ice layers have varying pressures and they tend to shift and move. Sometimes those chunks ascend to the surface, causing some rather dramatic plume events."

"Like a normal volcano?" Jason still didn't see anyone else in the room looking overly concerned. Several of the staff were laughing softly. *Must be a fairly common occurrence then.* It didn't mean that he was eager to sit through another one though. *Why the hell wasn't this ever mentioned?*

"Yeah, just like a normal volcano. Only instead of molten rock, this one is venting water, ammonia, methane gas, etc. Been happening pretty much forever." Mark reached for his bagel and took a bite. "Titan's sandy surface is nothing more than grain-sized ice and ammonium sulfate ash."

Jason reached for his half-filled coffee mug, wishing that he had something strongly alcoholic to add to it. "Do these cryovolcanoes happen a lot?"

"Often enough...no serious danger for us though. This area is pretty geologically stable." Mark gestured with his free hand. "You don't see the other pencil pushers in a panic, do you?"

"No."

"Then there's nothing to worry about." Mark shook his head, a faint grin on his face. "Yu-Wei really didn't prepare you guys for this place."

"No, the company left a few things out." Jason took another drink from his mug. "I'll have to mention this when we renegotiate our contracts."

An alarm sounded over the intercom speakers. Two hoots, followed by three, then two more.

Mark's face paled.

Jason frowned. *He didn't look that worried during the quake.* "What wrong now?"

"The Cradle!" Mark sprang to his feet, knocking his chair over as he did so. "Oh, God! Fiona!"

"What's going on?" Jason called out.

Mark ran through the cafeteria doorway without answering,

"What's happening?" Jason demanded as the alarms continued to sound the same series of hoots. Everyone else in the cafeteria had abandoned their breakfasts and were hurrying to their feet. "What's the worry? Mark?" Jason hurried after him.

Chapter Twelve

Feet pounding on the rocky floor, Mark ran through the roughly-finished corridors of Trove. He had left the cafeteria and headed directly towards the hatchway and bulkhead which normally sealed off the tunnel leading to the Cradle.

Jason ran after him. He ran past a handful of other researchers and technicians who were hurrying on their own duties. They all appeared to know what they were doing and where they were supposed to be. He also noticed that none of them stopped to ask why either he, or Mark, was running.

Jason rounded a corner and skidded to a stop.

The hatchway was already partially open and the rocky tunnel beyond was dark, with only a few widely separated lights hanging from the ceiling.

Mark Vance was backing away from keypad controls. His eyes were wide and he was still gasping for breath.

Jason felt the same way, though he wasn't gasping as quite as badly. *So much for Ian's belief that having us run through this place would get us into shape,* he thought. *I'm so exhausted right now, I couldn't lift a gun if someone really was invading.* Then he realized that he was shivering. "It's freezing in there." He could see his breath crystallizing in front of his face.

"The tunnel isn't heated. Never had to be."

Jason rested his hand on his pistol, though he wasn't sure how useful his sidearm would be. *What am I going to shoot?* He watched the hatchway finish opening. "So, Mark, why don't we—"

Mark plunged through the now-open doorway.

"What a minute!" Jason hurried after him.

The rocky ground was very rough—there had been no efforts made to smooth out the surface during the original mining and sealing—and he had to be careful not to lose his balance. The widely scattered light fixtures were barely adequate to the task of brightening the tunnel and Jason could only just manage to keep Mark in sight.

"Slow down!" he called out. "You're gonna fall and hurt yourself."

Mark didn't appear to hear him.

"Where does this lead?" Jason called out, between gasps for air of cold air. The farther the tunnel went, the more it curved and descended deeper into Titan. It was roughly oval in shape, with the floor somewhat flatter. The air was colder too.

"To the Cradle."

But that's over two miles away! "We can't run the whole way." Jason followed after him, his boots crunching loudly on small rocks. "It's too far. It'll take us—"

"Shit." Mark had reached the end of the curve and he had stopped running.

The ceiling had collapsed and rocky debris choked the tunnel from floor to ceiling.

"Crap." Jason stared at the debris. "We'll never get through this."

Mark was just standing and staring, his posture that of a defeated man.

"We'll have to go back for some proper equipment." Jason hadn't brought his pack on this run, but he doubted his usual field kit would have been suitable anyway. *A few grenades might make a difference...and they might bring the rest of the roof down.* He looked up at the curved rock. *It looks solid enough though.*

Mark pulled a loose rock away from the pile, and tossed it aside.

"Mark, that's not gonna work." Jason shook his head. "No way."

"Fiona is at the Cradle. She needs me."

"How do you know that?"

"I just do!"

Are you a teep? Jason wondered. He dismissed that thought just as quickly as it had popped into his head. *He's shown no ability to read anyone's thoughts. If he had any idea what I'm usually thinking about when he's around, he'd have punched me by now.*

Mark was still pulling at the rocks.

Two other techs arrived, panting and gasping, and they stopped once they saw the extent of the collapse. One was holding a collapsible shovel in his hand. The other was carrying a small tool-case in her hand.

"Looks like a pretty solid fall," the man with the shovel commented.

"You'll have to dig it out again," Jason told him.

The man shook his head. "This shovel isn't going to cut it. Sandra?"

"I didn't bring anything better," she replied in a grim tone. "We're gonna need some real tools for this." She set the tool-case down. "Mark, what's the rush?" She watched him, with concern in her eyes.

"Fiona's in this!" Mark had grabbed at a jagged rock with his hands and was trying to pull it loose. "Fiona!" he shouted as he struggled.

"She'll never hear you, Mark." The first technician pulled a com-link out of his pocket and held it up to his mouth. "Alton Jarvis here, Director. It's a rock collapse in the Cradle tunnel. Looks like a solid fall just past the first bulkhead."

Mark was still straining to pull loose rocks from the fall.

"Come on." Jason placed his right hand on Mark's shoulder. "Come on, before you hurt yourself. We need the right tools for this." He pulled Mark away from the debris, the other man struggling in his grip. "Explosives maybe."

"That would risk a further collapse," Sandra replied. "Mark, breath. Take it easy."

"But Fiona—"

"Should be in her shuttle, right? She never walks anywhere that she can fly."

Mark slumped, almost lifelessly into Jason's arms.

"Thanks." Jason gave Sandra a smile, then he pulled Mark back towards the main complex. He took his time, savoring the sensations of having the other man in his arms. *I can cop a quick feel too,* he thought. *Mark has a good build under his clothes.*

Mark was staggering along, as if sleepwalking.

"Everything's fine," Jason told him in the most reassuring tone of voice that he could manage. "You'll see. We just have to get back to the main complex and we can raise her on the comm."

The opening to the complex was in sight when a woman in white coveralls stepped through it. She was carrying a silvery pack in her hand and had another one strapped to her back. "Hello!" she called out. Her voice had a strong Spanish accent. "How badly are you hurt?" She eyed Mark's dirty tee-shirt and jeans with a concerned expression.

"We're fine." Jason shook his head at her. "We were both in the cafeteria when the tremor hit. We're not hurt."

"So what were the two of you doing in the tunnel?"

"I was chasing him." Jason recognized the woman now—she was Trove's chief physician—but he couldn't recall her name.

She frowned. "Cave-in?"

"Looks like it, Doctor." Jason paused. "He's just stressed."

"He looks like it." She had a portable scanner in her hand and was waving it in Mark's general direction. "So why are you so concerned?"

"Fiona made a run to the Cradle today," Mark said in a low tone of voice. "She commed me earlier that the shuttle was having some mechanical problems. She was going to have to walk back here to pick up some parts and tools. I was supposed to go back with her to help."

"Oh."

"She should've been here by now. She could be buried under all that crap."

"If she is, then she's beyond our help, Mark."

"Eloyda!"

The doctor shrugged. "Otherwise, she's still at the Cradle."

"She's no safer there."

Eoyda looked at him sharply. "In any event, you won't do her any good by worrying yourself into a heart attack, Mark. Calm down."

"No, I have to—"

"Don't make have to give you a sedative." There was a clear note of warning in Eloyda's voice.

Mark grunted, but stopped protesting.

Eloyda eyed him for a moment, then she looked at Jason. "How many other people might be hurt?"

"I don't know, Doctor." Jason shrugged. "Ian was supposed to accompany Fiona there on a tour. I think he took Brad Kellar, but I don't know who else was going with them."

She was nodding to herself.

Mark was looking frantic again. "We had that section under a tight containment. How could this happen?"

"It was just a tunnel collapse. We can dig down it out again, right?" Jason paused, looking back over his shoulder into the shadowy dimness. "Why are we even walking? You're a pilot. Can't you just fly out there?"

He shook his head. "The other shuttle is down for maintenance."

"Damn." *What a screw-up.* Jason pulled his own link out of his pocket and keyed it to the squad's usual frequency. "Sarge, are you there?" He only got crackling static in response.

Mark was staring at him.

"Come on, you stupid piece of junk." Jason adjusted the link, trying to tie it into the complex's more powerful transmitter. *These things are supposed to automatically make those types of connections.* "Sarge? You there?" There was another crackle of static. "Ian, reply please."

"*Yeah, I'm here. Damned tunnel collapsed on us.*" The link carried the full measure of his annoyance. "*Fiona says it looks pretty solidly blocked from this side.*"

Mark gasped.

"Is she okay?" Jason asked quickly.

"Bruised a bit. Crabby too. I think she dented one of her legs...and the warranty doesn't cover acts of God."

Mark was listening closely to the exchange. Now he chuckled. It was weak, but it was a chuckle. "That sounds just like her."

Eloyda was watching him closely.

"Who else is with you?" Jason asked.

"Just Fiona right now. We were using a small buggy to travel back to Trove...that damned shuttle broke down on us. Damian was right—it was a Mark Five—but don't tell him that. He'll be even more insufferable. Hang on. What? Fiona says there's likely seven or eight people at the lab. Not much staff out there right now. Just the normal duty roster."

"Is anyone else hurt?" Eloyda demanded.

"Not that we know about. We're still in the tunnel though. I left Brad back in the Cradle, before we left. Had to save space in the buggy."

"We're going to have to do some digging to get to you," Jason said. He could see other technicians hurrying past him into the tunnel with shovels and pick-axes. "It might take some time though."

Mark nodded, his mouth twisted sourly.

"No big rush on that. We can return to the Cradle from here. Fiona told me they have plenty of food supplies. We were carrying a bunch of it with us anyway. It will tide us over until you can rescue us. If not, we can always walk back."

"Walk?"

"The Cradle has a full complement of environmental suits. We can manage the two mile walk. Well, Brad and I can manage." There was a quick burst of muttered cursing from the link. *"All right, all right. The three of us can manage."*

"Do you want me to send a rescue vehicle? I can get a dust-buggy prepped."

"No need to do that. We'll be fine for now. Keep the others in line until I get back there."

"Got it, Sarge." Jason turned the link off. "Ian's gathering a team for a surface trek. We'll suit up and open up the back door as it were."

Mark shook his head. "It's a hell of a lot more dangerous that you think."

"We're trained for this. We can meet them partway."

"You're going *outside*?"

"How else do you suggest that we get there, Doctor?" Jason asked.

"The Cradle is under a very strict level of biological containment." Floyda Acuna wiped a sheen of sweat from her olive skin with her hand. "It's vitally important that the facility's containment is not broken."

"I'm sure that Ian will keep that in mind."

"We can send a *Mole*." Mark hooked his thumb in the direction of the vehicle garage. "We'll just carve ourselves a brand new tunnel."

Eloyda frowned at that.

"Come on!" Mark took off running towards the elevator shaft and Jason hurried after him.

Jason stared at the *Mole*. It was an elongated cone-shaped machine, with tracks along its base and a series of drill-bits around its front end. "You're driving?"

"Damn right I am." Mark was already inside the cockpit, fastening his seatbelt. "If you're coming, then you'd better strap in."

Jason hastily did so. There was only one seat, for the driver, but he found a place to squat in the rear storage compartment.

The vehicle's motor roared to life.

"This isn't going to be a very speedy rescue," Mark muttered as he adjusted the throttle and the *Mole* lurched into motion. "It's not a pretty machine, but it works."

Jason held on silently as Mark manoeuvred the *Mole* out of its parking cradle. *I hope he knows what's he's doing,* he thought. "We're staying underground?"

The garage had rough rock sides, pockmarked with unfinished tunnel openings and Mark simply drove into one.

"Of course I am. I can't drive this thing through a finished tunnel. It would smash all the ducting and lights."

"True." Jason could see that most of the facility corridors were roughly the size of the *Mole*.

Mark was driving straight towards a wall of solid rock. "Now we start drilling." He typed commands into the console with his right hand. "We'll dig down and link up with the existing tunnel." The drill-bits at the front of the *Mole* began whirring to life, creating even more noise.

"You can find it?"

"G.P.S. system. Impossible to get lost." The rock seemed to simply melt away in front of the *Mole* as the drills bit in. "Normally I'd be hooked up to a conveyor system to haul the tailings away," Mark explained. "But I'll just let the tunnel fill back up behind me. This one doesn't matter."

"I trust you." Jason had no choice really as the *Mole* chewed its way slowly through the rocky surface of Titan. The drills were screaming loudly and waves of heat from the plasma core washed through the compartment.

Jason felt like his teeth were being shaken clean out of his head. The drills were breaking up the rock and those chunks were was passing through the mining machine to loosely refill the tunnel behind them. *There should be another machine back there to fill up with our tailings,* he recalled Mark explaining. There hadn't been much chance for them to talk to one another, given the loudness of the drills and the rumble of the *Mole* itself.

In any event, Mark had not seemed interested in idle chitchat. He was staring through the windscreen with a worried expression on his face.

If it's this loud inside the insulation, Jason thought, *what must it be like* outside? Then he wondered if there was anyone else in the area to hear the noise. "Mark?" he shouted over the noise.

"Yeah?"

"How safe is this thing?"

"Perfectly. The technology goes back to the nineteen nineties on Earth. Digging out the Chunnel and the like."

"I meant—"

"We tunnelled out all of Trove with these machines."

"Yeah, but at the time there wasn't anyone else around." Jason paused for a long moment, feeling the vibration of the machine shaking every bit of him. *Like I'm riding some overpowered vibrator...figure out a way to market this thing and we could make a fortune!*

"So?"

"So you dug out Trove with these, right? You dug out the tunnels first and then moved in the crews. If we're just blindly digging our way towards an existing tunnel, then isn't there a risk we might run over someone?"

"No, I've been digging out a brand new tunnel." Mark peered at the controls. "The *Moles* broadcast a warning signal. Fully automated, to prevent killing anyone by accident. Anyone around will pick it up and hear us coming."

"Oh." Jason hoped he was right. "How close are we to the collapse?"

The *Mole* broke through into an open tunnel.

"There we go." Mark changed the miner's direction so that he was following the existing tunnel. He cut the drills. "The collapse is just ahead."

"Good." Jason breathed with relief as the noise dropped to just a dull rumble. The waves of heat were still making him sweat though.

"Almost there." Mark made an adjustment to the controls. "A few minutes more and we'll hit it."

"Anyone else around?"

"No sign of anyone."

"But there were techs at the collapse. I mean, they showed up before we left right?"

"There's no one registering," Mark replied. "The warning beacon is going."

"You're sure?"

"Yes."

Jason shifted position, trying to get more comfortable in the cramped cargo space. "Just go in slow, okay? Humour me."

"Fine." Mark sighed.

"Thank you."

Mark glanced back over his shoulder and managed a weak smile.

Jason took a deep breath. "So once we hit the rubble, we turn the drills back on?"

"Yep."

"Just like making that tunnel here?"

"Yep."

"And what about those tailings? I mean, we want *this* tunnel to be clear for usage by the others, right?"

"If I go slowly and crank the plasma to its highest setting, the *Mole* should able to clear the collapse and use that material to reinforce the walls and ceiling." Mark grimaced. "It's gonna pretty much drain the batteries on this thing, and it won't make the tunnel look very pretty, but it should work."

"You could call for a back-up crew to remove the tailings."

"There's no time for that. Fiona needs us right now."

A chirp sounded from the console.

"Yeah?" Mark asked after he hit a button.

"*We're loading up a buggy now,*" Doctor Acuna's voice came from the speaker. Her accent was made even worse by the poor quality of the speakers. "*We'll be following you to the Cradle once you get the main tunnel dug back out.*"

"Got it. Give me a few more minutes...I can see the collapse now." Mark turned the drill-bits back on. "Brace yourself, Jason."

"I'm ready."

The noise of the drills grew to almost deafening levels again.

The airlock room was large enough to hold two or three buggies. It was empty, other than the *Mole* and the buggy which had followed it in.

"Space is not at a premium around here," Mark muttered. His breath hung in the air before him. "We tunnelled out whatever we felt we needed."

"Why is it so damned cold?" Jason asked. He rubbed his arms, wishing that his uniform was either thicker or warmer. *I should have kept my winter clothes from my trip to Quebecneuve,* he thought. After the heat of the waste heat from the *Mole* Machine's plasma furnaces, the air felt colder than usual.

"Budget. Lower temps means lower expenses." Mark gave him a shrug. He rubbed his own arms. "I think Claire would turn off all the heating elements and just have us wear thermal gear if the chemical agents in the labs didn't need to be kept above freezing."

"Great." Jason keyed his comm. "Ian, we're at the hanger airlock."

The main hatch on the dust-buggy popped open and Eloyda Acuna carefully climbed out. "Claire is throwing a fit over your unauthorized tunnelling," she said as she dropped to the ground "We had to listen to her complaining about you for most of our trip here. She was quite annoyed that you were not responding to her."

"The radio on the *Mole* isn't too great," Mark replied with a shrug. "I've told her it needs some maintenance but she won't budget for it. Might lose her bonus cause of the *unnecessary* expense."

"Maybe I should tinker with our radio then." Eloyda hastily checked through her medikit and then snapped it closed. "But likely not." Her buggy was large enough to hold eight passengers, but only Terry Sisler and Joshua Warner climbed out. Both men were wearing their duty uniforms, with PPGs in their holsters.

"Everyone else is staying put," Joshua explained. "Franco and Damian are at the other end, guarding the tunnel entrance."

From what? Jason wondered.

"So what are we waiting for?" Terry asked.

"Waiting for the Sarge." Abruptly recalling the comm in his hand, Jason looked down at it. "Ian?" he repeated. There was just soft static. "What the hell?"

Mark had already hurried across to the inner lock. He punched his pass-code into the keypad and waited.

Terry frowned. "Nothing's happening."

"Can you hurry it up a bit?" Jason asked. "I'm freezing here."

"There's a glitch of some kind. The computer is under lockdown." Mark retyped his code. "Come on, you stupid thing."

Joshua poked Terry. "Guess I should have brought Damian along instead of you."

"Guess so."

Mark retyped the code a third time. "Damn it!"

Eloyda pushed past him. "Calm down, Mark." She keyed in her own pass-code, but the airlock remained sealed. "Odd, that should have worked."

"We've got to get in there!" Mark told her. He was rubbing his bare arms. "I can use the *Mole* to—"

"Calm down." Eloyda eyed him. "Don't make me sedate you!" she warned.

Mark closed his mouth.

"I have my own codes. Medical priority." She typed into another code. After a moment, the panel beeped and the hatch hissed open. "There we go."

Mark hurried through before the door had finished opening.

"Hang on!" Jason hurried after him. "What's your rush?"

The inner corridors of the Cradle were a veritable carbon copy of the main base. The corridors had been roughly tunnelled out of the rock, given only the most basic finishing. The ceiling was lined sparingly with cheap fluorescent fixtures which flickered and buzzed in a persistent and annoying fashion. There was exposed duct work and only basic signage.

Most warnings about entering a restricted area. Authorized personnel only. Jason stifled a laugh at that. *Who would be on this base if they were not authorized?* And anyone who wasn't authorized certainly wouldn't worry about warnings.

Mark was leading the way, with Jason close behind. Terry and Joshua brought up the rear, with Eloyda in front of them.

"Hey, slow down, Mark!" The corridor was quite dark, with only every second fixture actually lit up—and most of them were flickering intermittently.

The man looked back at them and slowed his pace just a bit. "We need to reach the facility," he said urgently.

"I thought we were in the Cradle?"

"This is just the access corridor." Mark was hurrying again, vanishing into the shadows. He voice echoed back to them. "The vehicle garage was built in an existing cavern. We just had to enlarge it bit. The main laboratories were built around another series of caverns and existing tunnels. A short walk, but less work overall for us."

"Oh." *And cheaper to convert as well,* Jason guessed.

"Awfully quiet, isn't it?"

Jason agreed with Terry's question. "Yeah, it is." He touched his holstered PPG, feeling the urge to draw and carry it ready in his hand. His boots crunched softly on the rocky floor. *At least it's smoother than that tunnel.* Which made sense after all. *Don't want the important researchers to trip and fall.* "Rather darker than what I expected."

"The lights aren't operating at full strength," Eloyda pointed out. She was panting for breath, clearly not used to keeping up such a fast walk for long. "It looks like the Cradle has gone into its power conservation mode."

"Why would it do that?"

"I'm not sure."

Jason eyed the doctor.

Mark was standing at a sealed hatchway. He was typing commands into the keypad and swearing loudly at the same time. "Damned piece of junk!" He slammed his fist against the wall.

"Mark!" Eloyda exclaimed. "Calm down." She hurried over to him.

Joshua walked over to the wall terminal. "Another airlock?"

"It's a well-sealed base."

"I *knew* we should have brought Damian." Joshua gave them a grin. He typed in a couple of commands. "The computer won't me increase the lights," he complained after a moment. "System is under lockdown."

"I thought there was a slight red hue to the lighting," Terry commented.

"Emergency status?" Jason turned towards his companions. "Why the containment, Doctor?"

"Potential infection," she replied after a moment. "The Cradle is dealing with the search for life. Finding new micro-organisms could lead to potentially fatal results for us. New germs and all."

"Great."

"If there was an infection loose, there would be a lot more alarms sounding," Eloyda reassured him. "We'd have been notified in Trove. Don't worry just yet."

"Too late for that. Doc, use your override and get his door open." Jason pulled out his comm and adjusted it. "Sarge? We're at the vehicle lock. Where are you? Ian?"

"Why isn't he answering?" Terry was frowning. "I mean, he can't have started walking back yet?"

"He might have."

"Unlikely, Joshua. He knew we were coming with a *Mole*."

"Fiona wouldn't walk," Mark said. "She hates walking. Even before her accident."

The airlock hissed open.

Jason stared through the opening. From all appearances, Cradle was abandoned. The corridors were lit with lights—these ones working considerably better than those in the access corridor—and every second fixture had a distinct reddish hue. "Mark, you're guiding me. Stay with me—no running off."

The researcher opened his mouth, but shut it again without saying a word.

"You guys, keep a close watch."

Terry and Joshua drew their PPGs. "Got it."

"Doctor, you stay behind me."

"Oh, this is ridiculous!"

Jason shook his head. He was surprised to see that he had already drawn his own PPG. *When did I do that?* "There's an emergency going on."

"Obviously...and that puts me in charge."

"Security outranks you." Jason held up his hand to forestall further protests. "I mean it, Doctor. You *will* follow my orders. Or you'll stay here with the *Mole*." He paused for a moment. "We can't contact anyone. There's no sign of anyone at all. Shouldn't there be some signs of activity?"

She nodded. "Yes, there should be someone around. At the very least, opening this airlock should have raised a flag in the computer."

"Something is very wrong here." Jason glanced towards Mark. "I suggest that we start with local Ops. Mark, lead the way."

"It's just down here."

· Chapter Thirteen

The hatch leading into the operations centre clanked open.

Jason winced at the grinding of the gears and machinery.

"Fiona must do the maintenance on it," Terry commented in a low tone of voice.

Mark shot him a nasty look.

Jason sighed and stepped through the opening. He had his pistol in his hand, ready to open fire at anything. "Empty."

At Jason's soft report, Mark immediately turned to leave.

"Wait a bit," Eloyda told him as she pushed him into Ops.

"But Fiona is out there somewhere."

"And so is part of our squad." Joshua hurried across the floor to one of the computer console. "We've got to find them." He sat down and started typing in commands.

Jason gave the room another quick look-over. It was small for a control centre, maybe ten feet by twenty, and filled with computers and equipment. The fluorescent lights set in the ceiling were glowing steadily, not flickering on and off, and the various terminals were humming softly. "Everything seems to be working." He slid his pistol back into its holster.

"Yep," Joshua agreed.

"But what about the others? We have to find them."

"We will, Terry." Jason tapped his comm-link and listened to the soft hiss through the speakers. "But right now our usual gear seems to be malfunctioning."

"Damned cheap contractors."

Jason ignored Terry's comment. "We haven't seen anyone since we got here." Their short walk through the corridors had been quiet.

"We haven't seen anyone!" Mark snapped.

Eloyda opened her mouth to say something.

"I know. Look, this is a control hub. We can access the facility's main computer to check the whole Cradle out. Right? It would be a hell of a lot faster than us having to go and check every room on our own."

Mark nodded, taking a deep breath. "Right. I'm not thinking too straight right now. Get out of my way, Joshua." He hurried across the floor to one of the terminals and sat down in the chair the soldier had hastily vacated. "I hope it accepts my pass-code."

Terry and Eloyda were standing next to each other now. They murmured softly to one another.

Jason gave the monitors and displays another study. Most of them were dark. "Can we get the security-cams online?" he asked. *This place must be wired. Most of Trove is wired up…I'd almost think management didn't trust its staff here.* "Mark, the cameras?"

"I'm trying to access them," the other man complained. "The system is currently locked down in security-mode. It doesn't like most of my clearance levels."

"Can you call Director Riley for an override?"

"Have *you* ever tried calling her for anything?" Mark asked in a dry tone. "Good luck with that."

"Damn." Jason kicked at the edge of a console. "What can you do?"

"What I already am." Mark continued typing.

"Trying scanning for life-signs."

"I know, Eloyda. I am, but so far the system is not cooperating."

"Let me take a look at that." Joshua leaned over his shoulder.

"We should call Damian in," Jason muttered. "He'd crack this place open in just a few minutes." He'd never seen a hacker anywhere who as skilled as Damian. *I'm just glad that he's on our side. I'd hate to be trying to raid a ship or base where he was running the computers and trying to stop us.*

A klaxon sounded.

Terry flinched. "What the hell is that?"

Jason put his hand to his chest. "Christ, that took years off me." He could feel his heart pounding. "What the hell triggered it?"

"Isolation breach. The Cradle is divided into sections." Eloyda gestured towards a monitor on the wall—it was showing a map of the facility. "There are twelve different pods, interconnected but still completely separate, just to be prepared in the event of a breach. Purely a preventative measure in case of—"

"Bio-warfare?" Terry spit onto the floor. "Shit! I told the Sarge I wasn't working anyplace with bio-weapons. I ain't gonna die from some strange alien germ."

"Shut up!" Jason snapped at him.

"Stupid piece of junk!" Mark hammered his fists against the computer terminal. "Where the hell is Fiona?"

"Where the hell is Ian? Or Brad?" Jason gestured at him. "Terry, access that computer. See if it will tell you something."

"We really should have brought Damian. This really is his thing." Terry stat down in front of the computer. "Maybe I can find the environmental controls. It's too damned chilly in here."

Jason agreed with that. *It is cold in here. Budget be damned, turn up the heat!* He leaned over a console. "I'm calling this in." He picked up a headset and slid it onto his head; it wasn't a *FujamiLink* model, but it operated on the same principles. "Director Riley, this is Corporal Shaw. Come in."

Static hissed back over the headset.

"Director Riley? Trove-base? Anyone?"

Mark was rubbing his arms.

"Nothing?" Eloyda asked him.

"I can't raise anyone," Jason told her. "I think it's transmitting, but we're not getting a signal back."

She eyed the console herself and then offered him a shrug. "It looks, to me, like it is working. Not that I'm a comm-tech, of course. I know how to operate medical gear...this is all pretty much beyond me."

Jason eyed another part of the console and a grimace flashed across his face. "If the Cradle has been invaded, I hate to broadcast our presence. Unfortunately, I don't see any other choice." He keyed the main intercom. "This is Corporal Shaw, Belt Consortium Militia...can anyone hear me?"

He could hear his voice echoing through the corridor outside Ops.

The others were looking at him and at the monitors.

Jason hit the switch again. "Sergeant Foster? Anyone? This is Corporal Shaw, Belt Consortium Militia...is there anyone still in this facility?"

"I'm getting nothing," Terry told him.

"Mark, you find anything?"

"I'm still looking. The system is taking a while to accept my commands." He was seated beside Terry, typing furiously at the keyboard. "Damned voice-controls are locked out. I have to do enter everything manually."

"Do your best," Jason told him. He dropped the headset back onto the console.

Eloyda had opened her small medikit and was looking inside it.

"What are you looking for, Doc?"

"Just rechecking my stock." She gave him a somewhat sheepish grin. "I just keep running inventory until there's a patient." She closed the kit. "Of course, I'm happiest on those calls when I *don't* have any patients."

"I can imagine why." Jason turned back towards the monitors. "Where the hell is everyone?"

"Must have called a meeting," Joshua commented. "Guess they forgot to tell us about it."

Jason rolled his eyes.

"The upper airlock is reading as sealed." Mark called up a picture onto one of the wall-screens. "The base is still sealed and contained. There're no records of the airlock opening in the last seven hours."

"Not since Fiona and Ian arrived?"

"Exactly." Mark nodded. "The shuttle umbilical is still connected. I see the log with the maintenance request. No sign of activity in the surface buildings. Even the power is cut back to minimal levels."

"Damn." Jason shook his head.

"The only activity I can find, so far, is us. The only airlock opening is when we arrived. The only computer access is currently here in ops."

"That makes no sense."

"I'm just telling you what the computer is telling me." Mark looked up.

"He's right." Terry nodded his agreement. "The only database activity is logged as Ops."

"This is a research facility...shouldn't there be other computer usage?"

"Most of the labs would be isolated systems. Data security."

"That is just silly."

Mark shrugged. "They do download back-up files to a central database to keep records in case of later accidents."

"How often?"

"Depends on the researcher. That would not show up in these logs though...we're trying to track info requests and searches. Automated back-ups aren't listed here. And no," Mark added, "I can't access those files to see when the last downloads took place."

"Damn." Jason had thought that checking the ongoing experiments might have given them a clue as to where everyone had gone. "Monitor the power flow throughout this place. Where are the current drains?"

"Aside from ongoing experiments?"

"Yeah."

"Let me check...."

An explosion rumbled in the distance.

Joshua whipped towards the hatchway and his PPG was in his hand.

Jason had done the same.

"What's that?" Eloyda asked nervously. "It wasn't another cryovolcano."

"No, it wasn't."

"PPG fire."

"PPGs don't sound like that, Mark." Jason stepped towards the hatch. He was breathing loudly and he tried to quiet the sound. "That was a lot louder." He was holding his pistol ready, though he wasn't sure what he planned to shoot.

"Power conduit I think." Terry shook his head. He was still seating, but he had swivelled his seat around. "Something blew one out."

"We'll have to find out what. Mark, hang on!" Mark was already halfway out of his chair. Jason shook his head. "Doctor, stay here with Terry. You'll be safe."

"There could be people hurt!" she snapped at him. "There should be over a dozen people working here. More if it's a busy shift."

"We'll call if we need you. So far, we haven't found anyone around. Nothing on the monitors either. No response to my calls or broadcasts. Now we hear an explosion? The Cradle could be under attack." *Though we've only heard one explosion. Not much of an attack is it?*

"Then Ops will certainly be one of the first places they look for."

"That's why you have a guard. I'd leave Mark here too, but I'd rather have a guide to show me around quickly. Terry, what do you have on the sensors?"

"Nothing showing up so far...no pressure loss or open airlocks that I can see." He was flicking through security camera feeds. "Not enough damned cameras though. Or not enough clearance for us at least."

"Pinpoint that blast. Joshua, you're with me. Mark, you're the guide around the Cradle. Let's go." Jason took a breath and stepped out into the corridor. "Just pretend it's a simulation."

"It had better be," Joshua muttered. "If this is some prank of the Sarge's, then I'm gonna kick his ass."

"I'll help you hold him." Jason managed to sound confident. *Please let this be a drill of some kind,* he begged. *Some grand test designed to drive us crazy.*

He had his doubts though.

"The company is definitely saving money on the power system," Joshua muttered as they crept through dimly-lit and cold corridors. They couldn't see their breath misting, but there was a definite chill in the air. "I hate outposts like this."

"It's company policy. The individual labs are heated as appropriate. So is the Cradle's lounge and the sleeping quarters. Why waste life support on the corridors?" Mark knew enough to keep his voice low. "Save what credits we can, right?"

"More light would be helpful," Jason muttered. He was holding his PPG ready for use, though he hadn't seen anyone or thing even remotely suggesting it would be a potential target. "It's hard to see what's at the end of this hallways."

"At least there's not much cover for invaders to hide in," Joshua pointed out. His coveralls rustled softly. He'd already made a comment about missing his body armour.

Mark shook his head. "The Cradle wasn't designed as a military outpost." He licked his lips. "This is crazy...if it was an invasion, we'd have been attacked by now. They'd be stealing the mainframe data!"

"Maybe...and maybe it's not another corporation. Could be aliens."

"We'd have been alerted. The orbital stations would have spotted an invasion fleet, or any approaching ships for that matter. There'd have been a stand-off. A fight of some kind. We'd have been warned."

"Depends on their stealth systems. We know that some of the aliens have better sensor tech than we do."

Jason nodded his agreement with Joshua. *A disparity which the corporations are desperately trying to remedy. The Guard would pay really well for a breakthrough.*

"If aliens slipped through, why bother attacking Titan? Why not go straight after Earth?"

"Looking for prisoners to experiment on?"

"Why bother?"

"Stow the guesses for later," Jason snapped at them. "Keep your mind on the here and now." He looked down a cross corridor. "Where did that explosion come from?" He tapped his comm. "Terry, have you got a fix on that explosion yet?"

"*Yeah, coming up.*" Terry's voice was clear in his headset. "*Power diverter blew out. Power was rerouted automatically. I see the repair request in the log now. Should be corridor five-one, near junction seventeen.*"

"So where the hell are we right now?"

"*Let me check.*"

"Five-two, junction seventeen." Mark pointed to a small sign. "Go right."

"Thanks." Jason looked around the corner. "Clear."

Something shrieked.

Everyone froze.

Jason tried to swallow in a dry throat as the shriek turned into an elongated hissing. "Pressure loss," he said, trying to keep his voice steady. "Bulkhead breach."

"That's no air leak." Joshua shook his head. "Totally different whistle when a bulkhead blows out."

"Yeah, but that's out in space," Jason reminded him. "We've got an atmosphere here." Toxic perhaps, but it wasn't a complete vacuum beyond the walls of the Cradle. "It must be an air leak." However odd it sounded. "It certainly wasn't another power conduit blowing out."

"We don't have a leak," Mark told them. "Titan's air pressure is one and a half that of Earth normal. It would leak *in*, but the samplers would catch it and sound an alarm."

The hissing had stopped.

"I'd damned well hope so!" Joshua exclaimed as he started to move down the corridor. "Hydrogen cyanide inhalation is not how I plan to die."

Something moved in the shadows up ahead.

Jason squinted. "I wish it was brighter in here."

"Me too."

Another drawn-out hiss sounded.

"Are you sure that's not a breach?"

Mark nodded. "Yes, I'm sure."

"There's something in there."

"I know," Joshua replied. He was aiming his PPG towards the shadows. "No idea what the hell it is though."

"What do we do?"

"Stay quiet, Mark." Jason was aiming his own PPG. "And pray that the other guy has worse aim." *Why* aren't *the lights working better? There's saving money and then there's just being stingy.*

Something was moving in the shadows...unless it was a trick of the light.

"I knew I should've grabbed my body armour," Joshua grumbled. "These coveralls aren't worth squat in a firefight."

"You and me both." Jason took a deep breath. *What the hell is it?* He couldn't clearly make out the shape in the shadows. *Could be anything.* He tightened his grip on his pistol. *Even our imaginations.*

"Do we charge or give them a warning?"

"It might a researcher," Mark reminded them.

"It might be a raider."

Jason tapped his comm. "Terry, do you see this?"

"Vaguely...the camera isn't getting a good look. You're almost out of its arc."

"Shit!" Jason swallowed. "Identify yourself!" he shouted.

The figure moved, stumbling into a pool of light from a bright fixture.

Jason got a half-glimpse of it and his heart jumped. It was no researcher, nor even a human being. Six impossibly spindly limbs attached to an elongated body which supported a freakishly deformed head. "Take it down!" He squeezed his PPG trigger and a burst of plasma crackled through the air.

That ear-splitting shriek echoed again.

"What kind of freaking body armour is that thing wearing?" Joshua kept shooting, but the plasma bursts appeared to simply deflect harmlessly away from the creature's glistening carapace.

"Some kind of robot? Terry, you getting this?" Jason listened to static hiss softly through his headset. "Terry? Damn it, answer me!" He fired again.

The creature stumbled towards them, darting from shadow to shadow. Its head was that of an insect, with black compound eyes sparkling dully in the corridor's artificial lighting. Mandibles clicked together in an ominous sound.

"Shit!" Mark muttered. He was stumbling backwards.

"We ain't stopping it!"

"I know! Reloading!" Jason stopped firing, then snapped the depleted cap out of his pistol and quickly jammed another one into place. "Fall back!" he shouted as he continued firing. "Maybe we can seal a bulkhead."

"Reloading!" Joshua called out.

Jason opened fire, sending more plasma towards the creature.

They got another half-seen glimpse of the thing as a light panel flared abruptly. It was walking on its back legs like a man. Its other four limbs were tipped with claws which it was slowly waving towards them.

"Next junction." Jason fired another burst. "Aim for its eyes."

"Easier said that done!"

"Do your best! Its head looks big enough."

"Steady retreat, lads," Ian Foster told them as he stepped around the corner.

Mark screamed at his sudden appearance.

"Continuous fire." Ian was holding a small canister in his hand. "Steady." He threw the canister towards the shadow-masked shape. "Target it and fire!"

Jason squeezed his trigger.

The plasma burst flew true and the canister exploded with a thunderous boom and that terrible shriek filled the air.

Ian slumped against the wall, exhaling tiredly.

Joshua stared at him.

Jason peered around the corner.

The smoke was clearing, being sucked away by the ventilation system, but he could plainly see bits of the creature splashed against the walls and ceiling.

"Holy shit." Jason felt like he'd been fighting for hours. "What the hell was that?"

"Good shooting." Ian pushed himself free of the wall and gave them a satisfied nod. "I should put you in for a medal."

"Where did you get a bomb?" Joshua asked as he kept scanning the corridor.

"Not a bomb, just a chemical canister. Contents under very high pressure." Ian had a bloody scratch on his face and his coveralls were torn at both the shoulder and leg. "I hoped it would be somewhat effective. I've been stalking it for a while now...I heard your broadcast, but none of the comms around here are working. I was trying to reach Ops, but that thing found me first."

"Where's Fiona?" Mark demanded.

"Where's Brad?" Jason added.

"I don't know." Ian shook his head. "We got separated when that thing first attacked us. That was hours ago."

"*Hours?*"

Ian looked at Mark. "We got cut off from Trove by the rock fall. We returned here to gather supplies and suit up for the overland trek back. Fiona insisted on eating something first. Most of the Cradle's staff were on break at that point. One of the researchers burst into the cafeteria, screaming about monsters and then that thing followed him in."

Jason shook his head.

"Brad and I shot it. Our PPGs had no effect. It clawed the researcher—I still don't know his name—and all hell broke loose. People scattered. Fiona was knocked down in the rush. Brad and I tried to maintain order. When we returned to the cafeteria, that creature was gone.

"And so was Fiona."

Mark cursed softly. He slammed his first against the wall.

"Someone triggered the lockdown," Ian continued. "Comms went down. We couldn't raise Trove. Couldn't reach anyone." He tapped his headset. "Someone installed a jammer—Yu-Wei really wants to keep the Cradle isolated."

Mark cursed again.

"The doors were sealed. Power was dropping to emergency levels. Brad and I tried to find the others, but we couldn't find any of the researchers. Just locked labs and personal quarters. No sign of anyone."

"And then that creature jumped you?"

"Yeah. Right out of the shadows. We'd heard your broadcast, Jason, and were trying to reach Ops. It dropped out of the ceiling onto us. Brad fired—hit something which exploded. There was a scream." Ian closed his eyes. "I couldn't find him or the creature."

"Shit."

"I head for Ops. Linking up with you guys was the best plan. I found that canister, figured I could shoot it and take out that creature if it attacked me." Ian gave them a sudden frown. "Where're the others?"

"Terry and Doctor Acuna are in Ops. The rest of the squad are back at the main base." Jason managed to keep his voice steady. "Only a few of us came out here."

"We have to rejoin them." Ian's eyes never stopped scanning the corridors.

"As easy said as done. We reopened the tunnel. Doctor Acuna brought a dust-buggy with her. It should be large enough to carry everyone"

"Good. We had a pair of bikes, but they got buried under the cave-in."

"I'm not leaving without Fiona." Mark turned away from Ian and glanced back towards the smouldering alien body parts. "Where did you last see her? The cafeteria?"

"She's gone. It was hours ago." Ian shook his head. "Feels like days. Damn, this place is a big freaking maze."

"Back to Ops," Jason said. "We need to regroup and rearm." He checked his PPG, then looked at Mark. "Two of us shooting and we didn't even slow that thing down."

Joshua pulled a spare PPG cap out of a pocket. "Sarge?"

"Thanks." Ian slapped it into his pistol. "Only had one shot left. Ran out of reloads a while back. That thing just kept absorbing the bursts. I might as well have been spitting at it for all the damage I did."

"What the hell was it?"

"I don't know."

"We can't leave Fiona out there. What if there's more of them."

"I know, I know. Come on." Jason grabbed Mark's arm and pulled him through the corridors.

Ian was muttering under his breath.

· Chapter Fourteen

The quartet stepped through the hatch into the small Operations room.

"Hopefully we can find something on the scanners," Ian was saying as he stepped through the hatchway.

"We've been trying that since we got here. No luck at all," Jason replied. He was still pulling on Mark's arm and the other man was cursing steadily. "The system is locked-down."

"You found him!" Terry was still seated at the computer terminal. He looked quite relieved to see the sergeant again. "What the hell were you guys all shooting at?" he demanded.

"Some kind of attacker." Jason shivered. "Looked like a man-sized preying mantis. Nasty thing." He frowned. "Didn't you see it?"

"No, but I could see you all shooting." Terry called up visuals from the security system. "See? Just shadows."

"Some kind of sensor cloaking?" Joshua shook his head. "Shit."

"A natural chameleon." Ian grunted. "Is the airlock back to the main base sealed?"

"Yes." Eloyda was standing near one wall, her open medical kit beside her. "It would have sealed back up after we passed through. Part of the lock-down procedure. Sergeant." There were two other men with her now, wearing rumpled clothing.

"We're not leaving without Fiona."

Ian ran a hand through his hair. "Doctor. Found yourself some friends?"

"Chuck and Tyler work here."

"We were down near the life support system when the evac klaxon sounded," Chuck said. He was the tallest person they had seen in the facility, and the top of his head barely cleared the hatchways. "We were heading to the garage when the doc flagged us down."

"Why didn't you respond to my earlier calls?" Jason asked.

"What calls?" Chuck asked him. "We never heard any broadcasts." Jason frowned.

"The bulk of the life support system is built deep under the Cradle...it's got a lot of heavy machinery and shielding there. Comms have never been reliable. Like Chuck said, we didn't hear anything until we came back out and then we heard the evac."

"You guys didn't see the invader?" Ian asked them suspiciously.

"What invader?"

"Big grayish-green insect alien thing." Jason didn't take his eyes off the monitors. "Really nasty." He realized that he was still holding onto Mark's arm.

Mark didn't seem to be complaining about it though.

Or he just hasn't noticed, Jason thought. He let go, with some reluctance.

Tyler was shaking his head. "Alien?" He had long, lank hair with a particularly greasy shimmer to it. His drab coveralls looked equally dirty and grease stained.

"Maybe it was a robot."

"Didn't look like any robot I've ever seen," Joshua argued. "It was moving way to damned fast and fluidly to be a robot."

"Might not have been one of ours. Could have been Dracos-built."

"Or Brokora?"

"Josh, you might as well call it an alien."

Ian shook his head. "Enough bickering. Joshua, take up sentry duty in the hall. Watch out for more of those...whatever the hell they are."

"Lucky me." He drew his PPG from his holster. "I *really* should've packed my body armour."

"Yeah," Jason agreed.

"But what about Fiona?"

Ian ignored Mark's question. "Jason, how long to get the rest of the team here?"

"Half an hour maybe. If we can raise them...comms seem to be intermittent. They keep going down."

"What?"

Jason hooked his thumb at the communication-station. "I tried contacting Director Riley earlier. No signal. I couldn't raise you either."

Ian frowned. "Our comms went down when the alert klaxon sounded. I thought it was a jammer to annoy invaders. I didn't think the main transmitter would be down too."

"It's part of the security system," Tyler told them.

"Great."

"Standard procedure. The computer has sealed the Cradle off entirely." Tyler stepped forward. "Let me take a look at it." He hurried over to the console. "I might be able to rewire it."

"Do your best. We need back-up."

"We need the frigging Colonial Guard."

"Quiet, Mister Vance," Ian snapped. "Get the comms working and call in the others. Tell them to bring their heavy guns. Doctor, can you do something about him?" He hooked his thumb towards Mark. "He's getting on my nerves."

Mark was still muttering softly to himself.

Eloyda sighed and moved to his side. She had her medikit in her hand.

"Sarge?"

"What, Terry?"

"I'm not finding any more of those things."

"That's good news. I only saw one of them...different places, but only one at a time. Maybe I killed it with that improvised bomb."

"Or maybe they just don't show up on camera."

"We saw it...it ain't invisible."

"I know, Joshua, but it was pretty hard to see in that firefight. There are lots of places around the Cradle which the cameras don't show. No coverage there."

"That's normal for high security lab," Tyler said.

"Is it?" Ian frowned. "I don't like this."

Terry grunted. "No sign of semi-invisible alien bugs. No sign of Brad either. He's certainly not invisible."

"I lost sight of him," Ian muttered. "We need to find him."

"And the other researchers," Jason reminded him.

Ian nodded.

"The whole facility is under lockdown." Terry turned back to the console. "The computer is not being very cooperative."

"So I gathered."

"I've got a question," Eloyda said. "Where the hell is everyone else?"

Ian flinched at her harsh tone.

"There should be a dozen or more researchers here. Where are they?"

"I haven't seen anyone else," Tyler commented. "Other than Chuck." He pushed his lank hair out of his face.

Jason looked at Ian.

Ian shook his head.

"No one moving around in any of the corridors," Terry told them. "There's no one anywhere that I can find."

Chuck was scratching his head. "They've probably taken shelter inside one of the labs. Once they're sealed and locked, those places are almost impregnable."

"Keep trying to contact them with the internal comms." Ian eyed the console. "I don't think anyone has left the Cradle. They just found a really good hiding spot." He tried to sound convincing. "We should be able to contact somebody."

Chuck moved to the comm terminal. "Let me run a diagnostic first. Maybe there's a short somewhere." He bit his lip. "Christ, I hope not. I don't want to have to go crawling around in the ducting again."

Jason checked his pistol, then holstered it.

"Well, Sarge?" Joshua stared at Ian. "What the hell was that thing?" He started as he realized that he had spoken more loudly than he had intended.

The rest of the room's occupants were staring at him.

"A Raider." Ian gave everyone a comforting smile. "Some pirate group are fielding a battle robot. Probably stolen from some alien merchant. It's obvious right? They'll use it against us cause we'll be scared of it."

Terry nodded. "We'll scrap it."

Jason shook his head.

"Do you still think this is the work of Raiders?" Jason asked in a soft voice. He looked around Ops, but everyone else appeared to be busy with self-appointed tasks.

"It could have been," Ian replied. Eloyda had found enough time to treat his injuries. Nothing worse than a few scrapes and cuts, which she had cleaned and then sprayed with instant-skin.

"I don't believe you."

"You don't need to believe me." Ian calmly took a bite out of a ration bar and chewed. "You just need to listen to my orders. Got it?"

"Yeah." Jason nodded. "Yes, Sir," he added after Ian glared at him.

"We need answers." Ian kept his voice low. The others were occupied, Terry and Tyler were trying to hack their way into the computer banks, while Chuck and Eloyda were scanning the facility with the security cameras. "We need to get some serious answers."

"I know, but the computers are—"

"Locked down. I know that. Once Damian gets here, he can play around with the database." Tyler had managed to get one comm-channel unlocked and Ian had called in the rest of his squad to help sweep the Cradle. "We need answers and I don't want to wait."

Jason grimaced.

"We need answers, Jason."

"I know that."

"We need to know where everyone is hiding."

"I know that too," Jason replied. *Assuming they are hiding.*

"There's one person here who can tell us more than he's letting on."

"Mark Vance." Jason heard the reluctance clearly in his own voice.

"Yes, he's worked here. He knows something."

"He's too worried—"

"Why is he so worried? Why is he so frantic to find that damned shuttle pilot?"

"I don't know. They were friends, from what I've heard. Maybe they were lovers. I don't really know."

"Can you get him to talk?"

"Maybe. Look, Ian, I—"

"What is it with you lately? Just get on with your job, Corporal."

"Yes, Sir." Jason didn't bother to mask the mockery in his voice. *Why did I agree to sign up on this mission?* he wondered.

Jason stepped through the hatchway and into the small room. "Not much in the way of privacy, eh?" he said. It was clearly designed to serve as an emergency office for staff members working in Ops.

Mark didn't say anything. He was just sitting on a couch and staring down at the floor, hardly even blinking.

Jason triggered the door and it hissed closed. *And that gives us as much privacy as we're gonna get.* He hoped Ian would stay away for a while. *I don't need him hovering over me right now.*

Jason sat down next to Mark. The springs in the old couch creaked as they adjusted to his weight. "Real stylish decor." The upholstery was a badly dated floral pattern. He clasped his hands together and rested them on his leg. His eyes struggled to trace the patterns on the rocky ground in the half darkness of the tiny room.

Mark sighed.

Jason shifted his attention to the man on his left, watching his expression through concerned eyes. "Hey, Mark. You've been in here for most of the day now. I wondered if you might want to talk, you know, about anything." Jason's gaze now wandered from the scientist's gloomy face to his chest, rising and falling with each silent breath. For a second, Jason wondered what he might find waiting underneath that tight, gray tee-shirt.

Mark finally looked up at Jason, a guarded look in his brown eyes and a weak smile on his lips. "Thanks," he said at last. "I guess I could use a little company. Have you found any sign of Fiona yet?"

Jason fidgeted with his hands. "No," he said, "Terry hasn't found any trace of her. Or anyone else either. Damian has been trying to hack his way in from the main base and he's pretty damned good at what he does." He shifted closer to Mark, reached out and put his arm around his shoulder, offering him some comfort. "But it's still too early to panic, Mark. Don't give up hope. Besides, Fiona can take care of herself. We didn't find any trace of her body after all."

"No, I guess not. But what if that thing got her?" Mark shivered.

Jason licked his lips. "It didn't manage to catch Ian, did it?" He wondered how much longer the sedative would last? *I don't want him becoming hysterical again.* "We got the comms working. The rest of the team is coming here, with heavy firepower. If there any more of those things around...we'll be ready for them."

Jason wondered if it was the way in which he spoke—soft and comforting, but still confident—which apparently made Mark feel better about the situation. Or maybe it was the sedative Eloyda had given him earlier.

Mark reached up with his own hand and put it on Jason's. "I know," he said, his eyes fixed on Jason's own blues.

"She'll be fine," Jason told him.

"I hope so."

Jason licked his lips again. "Why so worried?" he asked. "What's she to you?"

"Best friend." Mark sighed. "She was with me in the Colonial Guard. She taught me how to fly. We were both going to be assigned to the border...that first skirmish with the Takakas. We were gonna be famous. Gonna kick some alien ass.

"Then our shuttle got caught in a crossfire. Dracos raiders hit the Altair base. Some minor Clan looking to make a name for themselves. Settle a score with some other Clan. Nothing more than some stupid prank to them. We got caught in the middle of the firefight.

"We survived...but Fiona lost her legs."

"Shit. That's rough."

"I know. She survived and mustered out of the service. She got a civilian job as a shuttle pilot and I followed her. We ended up here." Mark leaned in closer to the man sitting next to him, and, in this dark, cold room, was fully consumed by the warmth that emanated from Jason's touch.

Jason moved in closer to the other man, his instincts taking over. He closed his eyes and felt the warm breath of the ex-Colonial Guard pilot on his face before feeling Mark's moist, red lips touch his. For a long moment, both men just sat there without moving, basking in the feelings that radiated from the point where their lips met. A beautiful, loving warmth rippling down from their mouths right to the tips of their toes.

Mark was the first to move. His hand rose up and stroked Jason's short hair.

Jason, suddenly feeling very reluctant, tried to pull back. "Are you sure you want to do this?" he asked. *God, do I ever want too!* But he was trying to remain professional.

"Yes." Mark pulled his head close and quickly shot his tongue out, tasting Jason's lips. He felt Jason part his mouth ever so slightly, and he eased his wet tongue between the other man's hot lips, swapping saliva, tasting the roof of his mouth, his teeth, and then Jason's own hyperactive tongue. The two men moaned lustfully into each other's mouths, and repositioned themselves on the couch.

Jason put one hand on the back of the other man's head, while resting the other hand on Mark's denim-covered leg, slowly gliding his hand higher and higher up the man's thigh until it was gently rubbing over the hard bulge that had appeared in his jeans.

Mark's free hand came down onto Jason's, causing the young security guard to rub harder on the growing pole outlined in the material of his jeans. "Mmm..." Mark moaned into Jason's now open mouth, as the other man gently suckled on his tongue.

Jason loved the taste of Mark's mouth, and was just getting into seriously sucking on his saliva-coated tongue when Mark pulled back, smiling and staring intently into his eyes, his hand still on the back of his head. Jason was just about to protest, when Mark laid a finger across his lips.

"I don't know about you, but I'm boiling. How about we get out of these clothes?"

"Uh, okay."

Mark smiled and ran his hands along Jason's chest, slowly unzipping the front of his coveralls, and bringing his trimmed, hairy chest into view. He started to lick and suck on his neck, hearing Jason moan softly.

Jason responded instantly. His hands lifted Mark's gray tee-shirt up, interrupting their kissing only long enough to pull the shirt over his head. He could feel his own hard-on straining against his boxer shorts.

Mark pinched his nipples. "Do you like that?" he asked softly.

"Oh yeah," Jason gasped.

Mark bent his head and started chewing on one of Jason's nipples, his thumb on the other one, playing with it.

Jason's own hands wandered their way along Mark's body, down towards his crotch. He felt the other man's cock move under his clothing. *I want this so badly,* he thought as he unzipped the jeans and reached inside. He felt his own coveralls fall to the floor.

"Nice," Mark murmured.

Jason could feel the hot breath on his skin, making it tingle with excitement, and then he felt Mark's mouth on his drooling cock. "Oh, my God!"

Mark could sense that Jason was on the verge of blowing his load, so he slowed down. "How far do you want to go?" he asked.

Jason looked down into his eyes. "We really...shouldn't...be doing...this," he gasped. "It's...not—"

"I want this," Mark told him. "I *need* this." He bent down again and took Jason's throbbing hard-on into his mouth.

Jason groaned, clenching his teeth to prevent himself from screaming out and broadcasting their activity to everyone in Ops.

Mark was massaging the length of Jason's cock with his lips, starting at the head and slowly working his way along the shaft. He tasted musky, almost sweet. He took one final run up the length of his shaft with his tongue before enfolding the head with his lips and drawing about half of it into his mouth.

Jason's moan was almost a helpless whimper.

Mark drew back so he only had the head in his mouth, then began curling his tongue around it again. He ran the tip of his tongue around the crown.

"I can't last for long," Jason gasped. "You're too skilled at this."

Mark grinned. "I'm badly out of practice." He wanted to make the most of these few minutes, so he kept the pace slow and gentle. He licked his lips, then gently slid Jason's erection into his throat as far as he could. He kept most of the shaft in his mouth while he began to suck him off.

Jason gasped as Mark's fingernails slid firmly yet gently along his goosebump-covered thighs as his body alternately tensed and relaxed in the depths of ecstasy. He was pushing his hips forwards each time Mark went down on him, and his breathing was getting unsteady.

Mark glanced up, just enough to see that Jason had closed his eyes, his tongue slowly tracing around his lips. Mark slowly increased the pressure he was sucking with, and his right hand drifted behind Jason's ass.

Just that faint touch of a finger around his hole made Jason gasp. It drove him wild. He was approaching the point of no return, and far too quickly. His breathing had gotten even heavier, and he was making whimpering noises, his body shuddering with tension on the verge of bursting loose.

Mark heard the other man let out a low, forceful moan. Then he felt Jason tense up and cry out. The erect cock swelled and then a sudden spurt was followed by a thick stream of hot, sweet liquid. Mark swallowed as quickly as he could.

Jason was panting for breath. "God, are you ever good at that."

Mark smiled and wiped his hand across his mouth. "You seemed to enjoy it."

"I did." Jason nodded. "What about you?" He reached down to grasp Mark's still-bulging crotch.

"I'm fine."

"Are you sure?"

"Yeah. I just needed...that." Mark slumped back on the couch, his eyes closed, and breathing heavily. "Now I really need a nap."

· **Chapter Fifteen**

Jason smiled nervously as he stepped through the hatch and back into Ops.

The rest of the people present were looking at him.

How noisy were we? he wondered. *We couldn't have been* that *loud. I hope.* He had taken a few minutes to get his uniform back into place and he was pretty certain that he looked presentable.

"What did you find out?" Ian demanded

Mark is one hell of a great kisser, Jason thought. "Not much more than we already know. The Cradle is self-contained and focused on research. Trove doesn't have much interaction with it, other than the occasional supply runs. This is a secret facility. Yu-Wei believes that no one else knows this laboratory even exists."

"All well and good, but what about that creature?"

"He has no idea what that creature was."

"You were in there for over an hour and that's all you found out?"

"He's upset. I can't just barrage him with questions."

Ian snorted.

Eloyda was looking at him.

"He's resting now," Jason told her. "He said he was tired. Your sedative—"

"Of course," she nodded towards him. "I am not surprised that it is taking effect."

Jason felt his face getting hot. *Damn it, I'm not a kid. Why am I blushing?* He really hoped no one had overheard him and Mark.

"Come on then."

Jason looked at Ian with a startled expression on his face. "Where?"

"The garage. Franco and the others are almost here. We should meet them and get ready to sweep this entire place. With some proper armour and firepower." Ian turned his head. "Doctor, lock the hatch after we leave. You should be safe enough in here until we get back."

Eloyda nodded. "All right." She glanced towards the office hatch. "I'll let him sleep off that sedative."

"Terry, you—"

"Are the guard. I know the drill." He tapped the PPG holstered on his waist. "I know."

"Come on, Jason," Ian ordered.

Jason followed him into the corridor. The hatch into Ops made a loud *clunk* as it closed behind them.

"So there's a new mission?" Franco asked as he stepped through the airlock-styled hatch into the access corridor. He was carrying his beloved *Mauser* CG-749/AC Heavy PPG Rifle in his arms and a bulging pack on his back.

Damian was also carrying a pack, but he let it drop onto the floor. "I've got it." He helped unfasten the straps on Franco's pack, letting it *thump* onto the floor as well.

"Search and destroy mission." Ian gestured to their surroundings. He opened Damian's pack and picked up one of the *Mauser CG-PR* PPG rifles the squad had brought with them. "We're going to sweep this entire facility for hostiles and eliminate them. And try to find Brad, of course."

"He's still not responding?"

"We're not getting anything from his implant," Jason replied. He was also eying the packs the squad had brought with them. *Body armour. Thank God!* "How about you guys?" He pulled on the torso plate and struggled with the straps.

"Nothing on this," Damian muttered as he gave the comp-pad in his hand a shake. "I mean, those things are supposed to keep transmitting all the time. Track you from orbit with the right frequency and gear."

"So why isn't he showing up?"

"I don't know." Damian rekeyed the pad. "Stupid thing."

"Could be some type of shielding. This *is* a research facility," Ian reminded them. He had also put on the various pieces of body armour over his coveralls, still struggling with some of the straps. "We're going to have to sweep the place, section by section."

Jason sighed. "There's a lot of ground to cover," he muttered.

"Finally." Franco was grinning widely. He was wearing his mission-scarred body armour and looking happier than he'd been since landing on Titan. "About freaking time we get to have some fun."

"Fun?" Jason asked.

"Well, a bug hunt is better than nothing."

"Oh, we're gonna have way more fun than you're expecting," Joshua muttered irritably. "Just wait 'til you see these bugs up close."

"That's why I brought out the big toys." Franco patted his rifle. "I'd like to see the raider who can stand up to one of these."

"Enough chatter," Ian snapped. "We're moving out."

The squad crept through the corridors of the Cradle. They had their weaponry ready for immediate use, their heads constantly swivelling from side to side as each of them kept a careful watch for more of the aliens.

The lights were fairly bright, but the temperature was still on the cold side.

"Can you see us?" Ian asked into his helmet comm.

"*Yes, we can,*" Terry replied. "*Nothing around you either.*"

"Still no sign of the researchers?"

"*Nothing.*"

"Anything from the surface locks?"

"*They're reading as sealed. No openings since long before you docked.*"

"Damn." Ian eyed his squad. "We're going to the upper levels. I want to check those airlocks myself."

"We're with you." Jason tightened his grip on his rifle. The rifles had been very welcome additions—they had longer ranges and fired a more much more powerful plasma burst than the pistols they'd used in their first encounter. *No WebCasters either. This time that bug is gonna go* splat!

Damian was eying his comp-pad. "Nothing showing up on my gear," he muttered.

"We're still close to Ops." Ian hooked his thumb towards the left. "We'll stop in there first and give Terry a rifle. Then we can head to the surface airlock."

Franco snorted.

"You got something to say?"

"Just find me a target, and then get the hell out of my way. Sir."

A faint smile played across Ian's face. "I'll bear that in mind." He gestured. "Let's get moving."

"You seem happy," Damian said in a soft voice.

Jason looked at him. "What do you mean?"

"You seem to be a good mood."

"Why would I be happy? We're being hunted by giant alien bugs. We have an entire research facility to check over. We've lost one member of our squad too. Brad might be hurt...or even dead."

"Yeah, but you keep breaking out into a really goofy grin." Damian chuckled. "You must have gotten laid."

Jason snorted quickly. "When would I have had the time for that?" he demanded. "I'm a little busy dealing with giant bugs, remember?"

Damian chuckled again.

The fluorescent light fixtures were blinking fitfully, casting the corridor junction into a collection of ever-moving shadows.

"We turn left when we get there." Ian was on point.

"I thought the lights were working?" Franco sounded annoyed.

"Could be a power surge."

"We hope," Joshua muttered.

Something hissed and the squad halted.

"Broken pipe?" Damian asked in a hopeful voice.

Jason shook his head. "Doesn't sound loud enough." He licked his lips. "Sounds a lot like one of those damned bugs." He lifted his rifle higher.

Something moved in the shadows.

"Stay calm," Ian snapped. "It could be Brad, or one of the researchers."

The creature stepped forward, into the steady light.

"Christ!" Franco swore.

It was a humanoid shaped bug. Its head seemed impossibly large to rest atop such a skinny neck, and its mandibles clicked together. Its grayish-green carapace glistened like the shell of a beetle, and its compound eyes glittered in the fluorescent lights.

"There's another one!"

A second creature dropped out of a hole in the ceiling and dropped to the ground of the corridor. It straightened itself up slowly and its mandibles clacked together.

Ian gestured. "Take them down!"

The PPGs hissed and the plasma bursts splashed against the creatures.

"We're not hurting them!" Damian cried out.

"Then we need bigger fucking guns!" Franco snarled as he fired his heavy rifle.

The first creature opened its mouth to hiss and the coconut-sized plasma bolt soared right between its jaws. Now the creature started to emit a loud shriek and the back of its elongated skull blew apart splattering greenish ichor on the walls.

"Yeah!" Franco exclaimed as the bug dropped limply to the deck-plates. "That's the way to do it!"

"Keep firing!" Ian ordered. "Watch that second one." His PPG burst splashed harmlessly against its shell.

The second insectoid chattered loudly and then spat something from its jaws.

Jason ducked as pale blue liquid splashed against the rocky wall near his head. "Damn it!" He quickly squeezed off a shot of his own.

Rifle fire increased as the squad continued firing.

The creature staggered backwards, towards the corner.

Jason frowned as he heard something odd. He turned his head. The wall was hissing. "It's eating through the rock!" he shouted as he moved away.

"What the hell?" Ian stared, then snapped himself back to the battle. "That's some potent venom."

"You're telling me."

"Its *spit* is eating through rock?" Joshua was reloading his rifle, swapping out the empty cap for a fresh one. "That's gotta be some kind of acid."

"That's impossible!" Franco snarled. "Nothing could live with that kind of acid inside it." He sprayed off a volley of plasma bursts but the alien twisted out of their path. "Damn it! Missed."

"He's right. This can't be real! It's gotta be a 'bot of some kind!"

The second creature hissed loudly.

"Cut the chatter." Ian waved them forward. "We can't let it get away."

"I don't think it wants to runaway, Sarge."

"Yeah, I think it wants dinner."

"Then we're gonna give it some serious fucking indigestion," Franco growled.

With reluctance, the squad moved towards the corner.

"I can hear it hissing." Jason licked his lips.

The creature leaped around the corner, its four claw-tipped arms held high and ready to strike.

Jason heard someone scream—he was afraid it might have been his own voice—and his finger tightened on the rifle's trigger.

PPG bolts splashed off the creature's exoskeleton. It swung its claws, gouging chunks of rock from the walls.

"Take it down!"

"Don't talk!" Ian shouted. "Shoot it!"

The creature opened its jaws and its mandibles loudly.

"We gotta get more firepower!" Franco snarled. "Concentrate your shots!"

The display of firepower grew more ferocious.

"Aim for the eyes!"

"We're trying!" Jason kept shooting. *PPGs are not known for their accuracy,* he thought irritably.

"We're not snipers!" Joshua snarled.

The alien let out one final shriek as its head exploded.

"Thank God!" Ian muttered.

Joshua screamed and collapsed.

"What the hell?" Franco swore.

"The torso plate!" Jason shouted and he dropped his rifle. "Get it off him!" The plate was smoking. He fumbled with the straps. "Shit, shit, shit!"

The plate hit the decking.

Joshua writhing. "Oh God!" he cried out.

"Get him back to the doc!" Ian snapped. "Fast! Franco and I will cover you." He kept staring down the corridors. "Shit."

"Hang in there," Jason pleaded.

Joshua was whimpering in pain.

"I'm on it. Hold him still." Eloyda Acuna grunted and held up the cauteriser. The pen-like device was a pale white in colour. "This will sting a bit." She slid her thumb over the trigger.

"God damn!" Joshua screamed as the instantaneous burst of heat cauterized his wounds.

"There, that will stop the bleeding." The doc slapped a patch onto Joshua's neck. "Just a shot of metazine to help dull the pain."

"Could—couldn't I have had...that before?" he gasped.

"No, I like to give it after I'm done. I prefer to have an attentive audience to watch me." She gave him a comforting smile. "It might encourage you to duck next time."

Ian left the medic and her patient alone and walked towards the rest of his team.

Franco was holding Joshua's breastplate by its strap. "Look at the size of that hole." It was large enough to put his fist through.

"Goddamn, he was lucky we got it off before it could eat all the way through."

Franco dropped the breastplate onto the table. "How the hell do we fight something like this? It spits on you and you die. Shit."

"Shoot it from a safe distance." Jason rechecked the cap on his pistol to ensure it was fully charged. "Better practice your marksmanship." His rifle was resting on top of a console.

Terry shook his head in disbelief.

"Just remember to aim for its head. The head seems to be the only weak point on those beasts."

"Fuck that." Franco kicked at the wall.

"Can't we clear out?"

Ian stared at Damian. "Clear out?"

"Yeah..." Damian swallowed. "Let's pack up our gear and go back to Trove."

Franco chuckled. "What, Dammo? You want us to take off and then nuke the site from orbit?"

"Why not?" the younger soldier demanded.

"Nuking the Cradle is not up for discussion," Ian growled. "The corporation would have our asses for that. The replacement cost of this facility is likely more credits than the lot of us *combined* will earn in our lifetimes."

"Only if we live long enough to spend them."

Ian glared at Damian.

"What are we gonna do about these things?" Jason asked. "We've taken out three of them so far, but there's probably more of them. They could follow us back to Trove base."

"Hell, they could already be there."

"Or waiting for us in the garage."

"No, if they were back at Trove, then we'd have heard about it." Ian tapped the earpiece of his comm. "Clair hasn't said anything last time we talked."

"How long have you been in contact with her?" Jason asked quickly.

"Long enough. And it's none of your concern, Corporal."

"All right then, Sarge." Jason bit his lip. *Just don't go holding out anything really vital on us.*

Tyler and Chuck, the two Cradle techs, were watching him.

"She never mentioned these things before either," Franco pointed out. "It would have been useful to know they were here."

"Maybe she didn't know about them."

"This doesn't fill me with much confidence." Jason rechecked his PPG cap.

"Don't panic just yet..."

"I'd be happier if we had the internal cameras working," Terry said. "I'd like to just what nasty beast is about to kill me."

"Tyler is still working on activating more of the cameras."

"He needs to work faster."

Jason walked across the deck. "What about Mark?"

Eloyda looked at him. "He should be awake by now. I've been leaving him alone, so that he could recover fully."

The hatch to the office hissed open.

"Speak of the devil and he appears." Eloyda hurried over to him. "How are you feeling?" she asked with quiet concern in her voice.

"I'm fine."

"Good." She was still studying him.

"I'm fine." Mark pulled his arm loose from her hands and he walked towards Jason. "You look tired."

"*I* didn't get to sleep the day away," Jason replied with a grin. "Some of us have to work for a living."

Mark glanced towards a chair where a bandaged-up Joshua was sitting. "What happened to him?"

"A run in with a pair of a bugs. We fried them—rifles can hurt them a lot more than our pistols did. Only, they can spit out this venom. Burns right through body armour like it was acid."

"Damn." Mark winced.

"We'll take a quick breather before we head back out," Ian announced to the room. "Break out the rations and get a meal. We'll need our energy for the fight."

"And my last mal is gonna be rations?" Damian groaned.

Ian gave him a grim smile. "Keep watching the screens. I don't want to be surprised while we rest."

· **Chapter Sixteen**

"How long can we stay here?"

Mark cleared his throat. "We only have access to a very limited supply of rations right now...unless you want to risk travelling to the food storage area." His face had more colour in it now than it had possessed earlier.

"We've got the firepower," Franco grumbled. "Be worth using it to get us some decent chow. A man can't live on ration packs. That shit tastes like sawdust and mud."

"You still ate *three* of them."

"I was hungry, Dammo."

"We'll have to go back out there if we're going to hunt down the rest those things." Ian looked back his squad, matching their blank expressions. "Assuming that there *are* more of them. We might have killed the lot already."

"We've only see three."

"Maybe there were only three of them."

"Could three of those things have killed all of the other researchers?" Eloyda asked. She was cradling a canteen in her hand. "I mean, they must be dead. There's been no sign of them. No contact at all."

"The doc's right." Tyler brushed his lanky hair out of his face. "Even if they hid out in a shelter, we should've made contact with someone by now. We've been running a lot of signals through here."

Chuck nodded.

"I'm inclined to agree." Mark sounded reluctant to say those words. "We should have heard something from anyone who's survived. Other than you two and the sergeant, no one else has been found." He glanced at Jason, then other towards Chuck. "The internal comms are working, right?"

Chuck nodded again. "Yep, but no one is answering."

"The Cradle is still securely contained. We're going to continue with our sweep." Ian clenched his jaw. "Any questions?"

"Why can't we fall back and reseal the garage airlock? We can guard the tunnel back to Trove easily enough."

"No, Terry."

Jason agreed with the others. "Ian, we could fall back to Trove, and then call Yu-Wei for more support. More troops."

"The nearest ships are days away." Ian shook his head. "We don't have the time to waste waiting."

"There are other companies on Titan, we could call—"

"Unacceptable. The Cradle was—is—a top secret facility. Exposing it to the other companies would violate its security. It would also invalidate our contracts."

"What kind of bullshit is that?"

"It's the legally-binding contract we signed, Franco. We stand on our own."

Jason shook his head. "Damn."

Mark put his hand on Jason's shoulder. "You said it."

Franco snorted and patted his rifle. "So we go back out hunting...and I'm gonna use this thing in its rapid-fire-mode."

Eloyda eyed the heavy rifle and then she swallowed. "Isn't it rather dangerous firing one of those things in here?" she asked.

"It's just helium plasma. No different to what our *Mausers* throw."

"Just got a bit more punch." Franco chuckled in his deep voice. "A lot more punch actually. I can fry a man wearing better body armour than what we're in."

The doctor's eyes grew wider.

Ian rolled his own eyes. "Any other suggestions?"

"No."

"So you have heavy firepower now. Boys and their toys." Eloyda gave her head a shake. Then she cleared her throat. "Did you try using morph gas on them?"

Ian nodded. "Yeah, the first time we got ambushed. Brad and I both threw grenades at the bug. The gas had no effect."

"But that's impossible...morph gas is used throughout the colonies. It's been used against the other races too. It affects everyone."

"Well it sure as hell doesn't affect these damned things!"

"Nothing that a bunch of raw firepower can't fix," Franco told them. "And I've got all the firepower we're gonna need."

"Pack up your gear and move out," Ian ordered his squad. "We've wasted enough time talking. We're heading out."

The two Cradle techs looked nervous.

"You have pistols and a lockable door," Ian reminded them. "Joshua stays here. He can fight if you need to protect yourselves."

Eloyda looked at her patient, before nodding reluctantly.

Ian checked his rifle. "Let's go."

* * *

The corridors were dim. Tyler had tired to increase the ambient lighting, but the computer was still not accepting most of his commands. "*I'm doing my best,*" he told them over their helmet comms.

Terry Sisler was on point, grumbling in the same way that Joshua usually did when *he* was on point. He kept swinging his rifle from side to side, watching for targets.

"We'll finish a sweep of this section and then seal the bulkheads behind us." Ian was checking his comp-pad, tracking their progress on a map. "If we seal off each section as we move through it, then we should be able to maintain a viable perimeter."

"But what about the life support system?" Terry asked.

"Most of the vents and hydro-tubes are too small for anything to crawl through," Damian replied. "I checked the architectural files."

Franco snorted. "*Most,* he says. Just miss one of them and we're gonna be eaten alive by those things."

"I doubt that."

"Nothing has tried breaking into Ops yet."

"True." Ian had left two rifles there, for Chuck and Tyler to use in case they were attacked. Joshua was with them as well, still being treated by Doctor Acuna.

Mark pointed to the next junction. "There's a lab just past that hatch." He was the squad's appointed guide. He had strapped on a chest-plate and helmet for protection, and was carrying a rifle.

He certainly carries the rifle like he's ex-Guard, Jason thought as he caught himself staring at the other man. *I bet he looks incredibly sexy in full uniform too.* He gave himself a shake. *Concentrate on alien bugs,* he reminded himself.

"Open the hatch then." Ian waved him forward.

Mark stepped up to the keypad. "Give me a moment then." He typed in a code. "There." The full lock-down had been cancelled, so now his pass-codes were working.

The hatch hissed open.

"Shit."

The laboratory was a mess.

Cabinets along the walls had been smashed open. Computer consoles looked like something heavy had been hitting them repeatedly. The walls and floor were stained with coloured liquids and substances.

"You can still smell it." Jason sneezed. The strong acrid stench of spilled chemicals was very strong in the air. "Is any of this stuff still active?" He looked more closely at the floor before he began walking deeper into the room—there were obviously sections which had been pitted and corroded.

Ian's boots crunched loudly on broken glass. "Is anything missing?" He spun around, taking stock of the devastation.

"Who can tell?" Terry slid his fingertips along a jagged slash in one tabletop. The ceramic surface was torn open, almost two inches deep.

Mark shook his head. "I have no idea what actually *should* be in here," he said. "I was never assigned to any of these labs."

"Damn." Ian was still looking around. "No telling where those things came from. No telling if anyone was in here either."

Franco was standing near the open door, keeping a watch on the corridor. He was patting his rifle in a gentle manner.

"The way he's stroking that rifle, you think he makes love to it?" Mark asked in a soft tone.

"You should hear him in a bunk," Jason replied in an equally soft voice. "He ain't gentle there."

Mark's face paled.

Damian turned away from a computer with a muttered curse. "It's wrecked. A total write-off. Something tore half of it apart, and then pounded the rest."

"No chance of repair?"

"Easier to replace the whole thing."

"What about the data?" Ian asked. "Can you recover any of it?"

"Not without hardwiring in another computer." Damian tapped the tools at his belt. "I doubt my comp-pad is up to it."

"Try."

"What the hell does it matter?" Jason demanded as Damian pulled out coils of wire and began to make the connections. "What's the point of trying to salvage the database? Can't we do that from anywhere in this place?"

Ian looked at him.

"I mean, we should keep moving. We have a large facility to search."

"The data might be important," Ian told him. "The computers in some of the labs are standalone systems. Limited access to prevent data theft."

"More insane security?"

"More protection Claire was very explicit in telling me about the precautions taken with some of these labs. There is a lot of top-level research being conducted in here. The Cradle could provide Earth with the advantages it needs to dominate the galaxy."

"Assuming that we live long enough to exploit those advantages."

"Jason, stop being so argumentative. Focus on your job, not on which guy you're planning to fuck next."

Jason blinked, startled by Ian's accusation.

The other squaddies were quiet.

Ian turned and walked to stand beside Damian.

Jason grimaced. He looked around, but Mark hadn't seemed to have noticed or overhead their altercation. *Thank God for small favors,* he thought.

The heavy bulkhead sealed off the corridor with a loud *thunk.*

"Locked." Ian clicked his comm-link. "Confirm that, Ops."

"*The seal is solid,*" Chuck's voice echoed back. "*Encrypting the codes now.*"

Lights on the small keypad flashed brightly.

"*Encryption completed. It's sealed tight.*"

"Thanks. Chuck. Nothing is getting into, or out of, that section." Ian hooked his thumb at the hatch. "Now we can move on and check the next lab."

"Great." Jason stood next to Mark. "Point the way."

Franco was still watching the corridor carefully. And still stroking his rifle.

* * *

"How many sections do you want to check?" Jason asked as a light-panel buzzed loudly overhead. "We've already swept three labs." He had florescent lights.

"And we've found nothing," Damian added.

"No sign of survivors, no sign of any more of those beasties." Franco grimaced at nothing in particular. "I'm thinking this whole sweep is a waste of time."

"You're not being paid enough to think." Ian had stopped to check his comp-pad. He read the small screen, then typed in a new enquiry.

"Do you guys smell something?" Franco asked.

"Just you," Damian told him. "When did you last take a shower?"

"Shut the fuck up, Dammo."

"Why aren't we hearing anything from Trove?"

Mark was leaning against the wall. "What?" He looked tired. He was also very pointedly *not* looking at the claw-like slashes in the wall and floor.

"Why aren't we hearing anything from Trove?" Jason repeated. "Shouldn't Director Riley be concerned with our progress?"

"She only cares about credits."

"Then she should be concerned that all of the staff here have vanished. Shouldn't she?"

Ian returned the pad to his pocket. "We're finish one more section, and then fall back to Ops to rest." He knew he could only push his team so far before they got tired and sloppy. "Move on."

Damian and Terry stepped around the corner.

The trio of alien bugs shrieked and leaped forward.

Terry only managed a partial scream before a claw of hardened chiton sliced through his torso-plate. He collapsed to the deck, gasping and moaning.

"Fuck!" Franco triggered his heavy PPG and a burst of superheated helium struck the blood-streaked monster.

Damian threw himself backwards as a second creature slashed at him. He scuttled backwards on the deck.

The glistening grayish-green carapaces gleamed as plasma bursts flashed past them. Their compound eyes glittered. One of them hissed loudly.

Jason squeezed off a shot from his rifle and he heard Mark's rifle echo his own.

Franco was still firing his rifle at a higher rate.

One creature jumped impossibly high, its claws smashing through the light-panel as it clung to the ceiling. Sparks rained down from the fixture.

"Check on Terry!" Ian shouted. He was firing his own rifle at the one on the ceiling.

Part of the floor erupted upwards, as a fourth creature clawed its way into sight. It pulled itself clear of the jagged-edged hole and clacked its mandibles together.

"There's another one!" Damian had finally managed to regain his feet, firing his own rifle at it.

"Shit, shit, shit!" Franco kept a steady string of curses and PPG bursts. "Reloading!"

Mark fired at the newest arrival while Franco hastily swapped ammo-clips.

The alien lost one of its limbs, but it kept coming. Greenish ichor dripped from the now-missing limb.

Franco shifted his aim and coconut-sized plasma bursts slammed through the creature's carapace. It dropped to the deck.

"Reloading!" Jason called out as he swapped out the empty ammo-clip for a fresh one. A foul smell wafted around them. *Like a back-up sewer,* he thought.

Ian shot the creature crawling along the ceiling. More sparks rained down from the smashed light fixture.

More of the bugs were climbing through the hole and Mark shouted a curse of his own as he fired repeatedly.

"Reloading!" Franco shouted as his heavy rifle fell silent again.

Jason grunted. *Twenty-four rounds doesn't last as long as I want it too!* He was impressed at just how rapidly Franco could cycle through a clip.

Franco yanked the depleted ammo-clip from his *Mauser* CG-749 Heavy PPG rifle and let it drop to the deck. He slapped a fresh clip into place and sprayed the bugs again. "Eat hot plasma death, bastards!" he shouted.

Another one fell.

"Terry!" Jason threw himself forward—the renewed burst of heavy fire from Franco only narrowly missing him—and grabbed at Terry's out-stretched arm.

The creature grasping Terry's legs hissed at him loudly.

Jason pulled, staring at the alien's glittering eyes and the two claw-tipped limbs it was lifting into striking position. The bug's mandibles opened and Jason abruptly recalled their ability to spit acidic venom.

Plasma bursts slammed into its compound eyes and out through the back of its elongated head.

Jason gagged at the stench of roasted insect.

Ian grabbed his arm and pulled him to his feet. "Leave him!" he shouted over the sounds of battle.

"We can't!"

"He's dead."

Jason looked. Terry's face was bloodlessly pale...and his body had been torn in half. "Shit!"

"Retreat!" Ian called out. He kept firing. "Now!"

Franco kept up a heavy rate of fire. "I can't do this forever!" he shouted.

With a hissing shriek, one of the mantis-like insects dropped from the ceiling and knocked Ian to the deck.

"Shit!" Franco was firing down the corridor.

"Ian!"

"Grab him!" Damian was firing his rifle as the bugs.

Jason struggled forward. "Ian?" The sergeant's body wasn't moving.

"Come on!" Mark grabbed Jason and yanked him backwards.

Jason struggled to break free. "We can't leave them!"

Franco kept firing. "We're not staying here!" His rifle fell silent.

Damian hit the keypad and a heavy hatch slammed closed, sealing the hallway behind them.

"Shit."

"That was one fucking disaster." Franco had reloaded his *Mauser CG-749* with a fresh clip. "We do *not* have the firepower for this kind of shit."

Jason was shaking his head.

Mark patted him on the shoulder.

"We gotta rethink this." Damian looked at the others. "I mean, we seriously gotta rethink this whole strategy. That first one just cut through the armour like it was foil." He tapped his own torso-plate. "These are supposed to protect us from shit like that."

"We need a lot more firepower, right?"

"And reinforcements."

"Before we *all* get ourselves killed?" Jason mechanically reloaded his rifle.

"How many of those damned things did we just kill?" Franco eyed the hatch. There was no evidence that the bugs were able to either open it or break through, but he was still watching it carefully.

"Come in. Ian? Jason?"

Jason tapped his helmet to active its built-in comm. "Go ahead, Ops." He tried to put some emotion into his voice, but he could not really be bothered.

"What's happening out there?" Joshua demanded. *"We're hearing weapons fire on the mikes. The internal sensors spiked on the heat."*

"We just got our asses kicked." Franco broke into the transmission. "Do you copy that, Joshie? Ian and Terry are dead. We ran."

"*Shit.*"

"You said it."

"Shut up, Franco." Jason felt Mark's hand on his arm. He gave the other man a quick glance. "Josh, are those bugs showing up on the sensors?"

"*Nope.*"

"So what do you see in our area?"

"*You guys in section nine-three. An unexplained heat source in section nine-four.*"

Jason eyed the hatch. "They came out of the floor."

"*Let me check the building plans.*"

"Hurry up. I don't want to have any of them popping up out here."

Franco eyed the floor with wide-eyes. "Shit!" He scrambled back to his feet, swinging his rifle downwards.

Mark was frowning, obviously lost in thought.

"*The only thing I see is part of the life support system. Hydro-tubing.*"

Mark nodded. "I thought so."

"*The tubing doesn't run under your section,*" Terry continued. "*You should be safe enough.*"

"Track the tubing, tell me where it does go. Like near Ops?"

"*Shit. Hang on a sec.*"

Jason eyed the others as they waited.

Mark was shaking his head, his eyes half-closed. He was muttering softly to himself too. "Not good, not good, not good."

"What is it?" Jason asked him.

"We're fighting bugs, right?"

"Yeah. That's as good a name as any right now."

"And when you have an infestation, you usually have a nest."

"Yeah," Franco nodded. "That's where the queen is." His jaw dropped. "Fuck me."

"Yep." Mark nodded. "Something has to be laying eggs and breeding these things."

"So you're saying we have a central nest?" Jason shook his head. "A whole nest of those things? We are *so* screwed right now."

"And the queen is usually a lot bigger than the drones."

"You're just full of good news, aren't you? That's usually Damian's job."

Damian gave a start. "Sorry."

"So if there's a nest in here, where would it be?" Jason managed a weak smile. "So that we know exactly where *not* to go."

"There's a lot of base we haven't explored yet."

"*Jason?*"

Jason jumped at the sudden voice. "Yeah, Josh?" he said, feeling his heart nearly burst. *Damned speakers are turned too high.* He adjusted them.

"*Tyler was running some resource consumption scans. There is a slow drain showing up in the recycling system.*"

"There is?"

"*Yeah, but we can't tell exactly where. Tyler is working on it. He says it could just be a slow leak.*"

Jason shook his head. "It's gonna be more than a leak, if Mark is right."

"*The nest?*"

"The nest."

"I bet I know where it is." Mark took a deep breath. "If we have a drain, then we can narrow it down. But my guess...is in the core of the life support systems."

"Oh, wonderful."

"How do you know?" Damian asked.

"Couldn't you smell it?" Mark demanded.

"What?"

"When they ambushed us? The ones coming through the floor? They smelled like they were coming from the sewage reclamation."

"Oh great," Franco swore. "I am *not* going down into that."

"Fantastic." Jason shook his head. "This just gets better and better."

Mark nodded. "Someone is gonna have to go down in there and investigate."

Jason swallowed.

· Chapter Seventeen

Jason kept a firm grip on the rifle in his hands. "Hurry it up," he ordered the others. Part of him still wasn't sure that he believed that he was actually doing this.

"I'm working as best I can." Mark typed another series of commands into the computer terminal. "It's not something I can rush. I have to shut down several automated systems and activate the various fail safes."

This is not going to be pleasant, Jason thought. "How much longer?"

"I don't know. I don't want to rush too much. If I miss a trigger, we might get flushed into the reclamation tanks. Or dumped into the incinerator." Mark licked his lips nervously. "That's not how I want to die."

"Duly noted. Take your time then." Jason looked up towards the door. Beyond that door was a very short corridor leading to Operations where the rest of the squad would be holding up. *Until we either isolate the nest...or until we get ourselves killed.*

Tyler was muttering softly under his breath as he checked a wall-mounted display.

"What are you so nervous about?" Jason asked. "*You* aren't going in there."

"No, but those bugs are in there. What if they're waiting on the other side of this hatch?"

"Then we're gonna have to start the firefight ahead of schedule." Franco chuckled and patted his heavy rifle. "Don't worry, techie, I've got more than enough firepower to fry anything which comes through that hatch."

Tyler swallowed.

"We'll be ready to help cover you guys too," Franco added. "We gotta avenge the Sarge."

"Yeah, I know that." Jason checked through his coverall pockets again. He was carrying plenty of reloads for his rifle, plus a few grenades. "I feel for the Sarge too." *Ian, this isn't how I wanted to see our friendship end. Maybe I should have stuck by you...but you didn't send me the right signals back.*

Jason gave himself a shake.

Tyler was still eying the hatch nervously. "They might swarm us."

"That's why you have Joshua, Damian, and Franco for protection."

"You sure about this?" Damian asked in a soft tone. He was standing near the doorway back to Ops. "I mean, we could just retreat back to Trove. Seal all the tunnel bulkheads as we go and leave this place for a real military team to clean out."

"Assuming that Yu-Wei would even allow the Colonial Guards to come in here, that is." Mark shook his head. "They'd send in more of their own internal security. Or they'd be a lot more likely to just hire more mercenaries—like you guys."

"Lucky us," Jason muttered.

"We're not mercenaries." Franco thumped his chest with his first. "We're militia."

Damian rolled his eyes.

"We're gonna get ourselves killed." Jason clamped his lips together, hoping that no one had overhead him. *Think positive. We are going to come back from this alive and well.* He glanced at Mark. *And then I am gonna fuck him senseless.*

Mark looked up and glanced towards Jason. He smiled weakly.

"So what are you hoping to do with this excursion?"

Jason looked at Tyler. "Check and see if there really is a nest down there. Maybe there isn't. Maybe we have already killed the lot of them." He doubted it though. "If there is a nest...then we need to try and figure out just how many more of these things are still kicking. Trap them if we can. Kill them if possible."

"So why not just trigger the lab's failsafe?"

Jason looked at Tyler with a frown.

"This is state-of-the-art research facility. There's a failsafe to destroy everything in case of extreme containment breach." Tyler wiped the lanky hair away from his eyes. "I'd call this whole thing *extreme*."

"So would I," Jason muttered. "Damn it, Ian, why'd you die on me?" That last part was said too softly for the others to hear. "However much we might want too, we can't just blow up the Cradle...Ian was right about that. The investment in credits and resources is very high. The company would have our heads." *But if the infestation gets any worse, then I'll blow this place and the company be damned!* He would not allow the bugs to spread beyond Titan.

A soft click sounded from the wall and a hatch burst open.

"Yech!" Mark grimaced as the stench washed over him. "It does smell worse than I remember."

Jason gagged on the smell. *Yep, this trek is going to be really unpleasant.* He looked at Mark. "You've been in there before?"

"Maintenance checks...basically it was a punishment detail."

"Hey, we didn't enjoy going in there either, buddy." Tyler shook his head. "Even with full environment gear."

"The tunnels are too narrow for full gear," Damian said.

Jason grimaced. "I know." Damian had called up the schematics and loaded them on his comp-pad. "It would have been nice to have been able to wear the suit though." The Militia favoured the *WY-2/ BX Hostile Environmental Armour*, as did the Guard. "Ian made us run around this damned whole base wearing that crap."

"No room for full suits." Tyler shrugged. "We made do."

"Hot shower afterwards," Jason muttered. "Really hot shower."

"The system is pressurized and the oxygen content is high enough for us to breath." Mark wrinkled his nose again. "We'll just wish that we weren't able to smell it."

"Lucky us." Jason paused for one last wish for even the helmet of his *HEA. But it's back at Trove in our lockers. If we go back to get it, then we'd just as well stay there. We need to do this sweep now.* He looked at Mark. "Let's go."

"All right." Mark finished checking his borrowed gear and weaponry, and then he climbed through the hatch. "Let's get this over with."

Jason grimaced as his boots squished through semi-liquid gunk. "What is this crap?" The smell was every bit as bad as he had expected it to be. Having to walk stooped over due to the cramped size of the tube did not improve matters.

"You don't want to know." Mark squished his own way forward. The light attached to his helmet illuminated their way clearly enough. "Just be glad the main carrier tubes are big enough to stand up in...you could be crawling on your belly through this."

"Yeah, I'm real thankful for that."

Mark walked on, slowly picking his way through the tube. He was halfway up his legs in the dark muck was, soaking his jeans. A few missteps had sent splashes reaching his waist. "Some of the smaller feeder tubes are less than half a foot in diameter. We have to rely on main bots for repairing them."

Jason muttered a curse. The air was damp and surprisingly warmer than he had expected it to be. The smell, of course, was worse than he had hoped. "How many of these big tubes are there?"

"Just four, coming from the various labs. They all join into one which empties into the containment tank." Mark took another careful step. "I've disabled the whole system for now. We shouldn't have to worry about any flash floods."

"That's a relief." Jason eyed one of the smaller tubes which was currently hanging over his head. "A real relief." He was soaked well past his knees already as well and he doubted that he would be able to get his uniform cleaned well enough to ever get rid of the smell. *I might just have to burn it after this.* He kept his rifle clear of the surface. *These things are rated for use under extreme conditions. I'm not sure if being submerged in sewage will wreck them or not.* He hoped not.

Mark glanced at him, relying on the ambient light from his helmet light.

Jason tried to give him an encouraging smile. *I wonder if the bursts from our PPGs will ignite the methane in here? Now that would be a crappy way to die.* He sincerely hoped the air in the tubes was not flammable.

They tried to move as quietly as they could, but it wasn't easy in the knee-deep muck.

"I do not want to slip and fall," Jason muttered to himself.

"Just take your time." Mark stumbled, but caught himself.

Hot shower, Jason thought. *Really long and really hot shower after this.* He glanced at Mark again. *With him to scrub my back....*

Mark stopped.

Jason looked up. They had reached a junction of pipes. Most were too small for either of the two men to make use of. "So now where? Not upwards, right? We can't even crawl through those."

"No, we want to keep going straight." Mark pointed. "Down there."

Jason aimed his light ahead. "It looks the same." All the tunnels looked the same. Seamless plastic, less than three feet in diameter.

"I told you the *HEA* would never fit through here."

"Yeah, I see that now." Jason grimaced. "I can still smell this place. I thought my nose would have died by now."

"No such luck." Mark managed a weak smile. "No sign of the bugs yet either."

"Yeah, good thing. Hardly enough room in here for a firefight." Jason didn't trust his footing in this foul-smelling muck. *One sudden start and we'll be underwater.* He tapped his helmet. "You guys reading us?"

"*Listening to your every word,*" Damian responded over the comm. "*Sounds like we're missing quite the scenic tour.*"

"You can have my ticket for the next time." Jason swung his rifle around as he heard a soft plop. His helmet flashlight skimmed the surface, but he didn't see anything.

"What is it?" Mark asked.

"I thought I heard something."

"Like what?"

"I'm not sure. A plop. Something hitting the water." Jason kept looking around, but he didn't see anything. "Are you sure you disabled the system?"

"Yes, of course I am. I don't want shit raining down on me." Mark looked up at an open pipe. "There might be the odd thing up caught up on something and finally falling. You must have heard that."

"If you say so." Jason took a deep breath, and instantly regretted it. "Let's keep moving."

They splashed on, deeper into the tunnels.

"If you breath through your mouth, the smell isn't so bad."

Jason glared daggers at Mark's back.

"We should be almost to the tank." Mark was oblivious to the glare. "Then we can go back and get out of this—"

"What the hell?" Jason swore as he stumbled.

Mark looked back at him. "What?"

Jason stooped and picked something out of the muck. He stared at it in shock.

Mark closed his eyes.

"Shit." Jason let the prosthetic leg slip back into the semi-solid muck. "I'm sorry, Mark." He reached out to grip the other man's shoulder.

Mark shook his hand loose and trudged on.

Jason looked back at where the leg had sunk. *Shit,* he thought. *Poor Fiona.*

"It's getting warmer in here."

Jason pulled out a small comp-pad from his belt. "Eighty-five degrees," he said as he checked the screen. "The oxygen content is dropping too. Higher than usual amounts of trace gases."

"We *are* in a sewage tube."

"I mean, higher than that should account for." Jason swallowed. "We're okay for now, but if the levels rise too much, we'll need breathers. We'll have to go back for our *HEA*." He hated to consider about having to backtrack so far. *I don't think I can convince myself to come back down here again.* No, he was pretty sure about that. *This is a one-time only trip.* "What's that on the walls?"

"I have no idea." Mark was frowning as he leaned closer.

It certainly wasn't natural. The normally smooth tube walls were now rough and mostly hidden by those oddly translucent coils.

Jason touched one of the looping swirls. "Plastic, isn't it?"

"Some kind of resin I think." Mark moved his helmet so the light would track. They both studied the looping whirls of the resin covering the inside of the tube.

"It's not natural."

"No." Mark shook his head. "It's not part of the system."

"So what is it?"

"I have no idea. It's not natural build-up."

"*Can you get me a closer visual?*" Damian asked.

"This is what I see," Jason replied. "The cameras on these helmets are crap."

"*I know. Hang on a moment.*"

Jason and Mark exchanged glances.

"*The doctor would like you to bring her a sample.*"

"We're a bit busy watching for bugs," Jason replied. "This is not a sample-gathering mission."

"*It could be important though,*" Eloyda's voice crackled over the comm. The poor connection did not mask the curiosity in her voice. "*It is very likely a product of your bugs. Studying it could be useful later.*"

"Listen, Doc, *you* can come back for a sample later. After we will kill the bugs. We don't have the gear to taken a sample anyway." He shook his head. "I'm prefer not to chip away it with my combat knife. What if it's hollow? It might contain a toxic gas."

"Or more of that acidic venom," Mark added.

"*Good point,*" Eloyda said in a subdued tone of voice. "*I hadn't thought of that.*"

"Well I did."

"*So now what?*" Joshua prompted.

"We're moving on," Mark replied. "We're almost to the holding tank."

"One other good piece of news," Jason added. "My sense of smell finally died."

Mark looked at him with a grin.

"About time too."

The tube opened up into a large open pit. Liquid gurgled from other tubes and pipes which lined the upper perimeter of the opening. The walls were lined with resinous coils and swirls, converting the machinery into alien architecture.

"Storage tank," Mark said. "To begin filtering the water."

"So we definitely don't want to lose our balance and fall in." Jason looked around. The surface of the pool looked solid, but he knew better than to trust that impression. *Be like falling into quicksand I bet.* "Is there a ladder? Or do we just jump?"

"There should be a ladder on the wall. For maintenance use."

"I so do not envy the maintenance staff in this place. Whatever the company pays them, it's not enough." Jason swung his helmet light around. "Where is that damned ladder?"

"Look out!" Mark shouted.

The grayish-green insect blended into the resin almost perfectly. Its jet-black compound eyes glittered as it slowly unfolded itself from a niche in the wall.

"This is for Fiona!" Mark triggered his rifle.

The plasma burst crackled through the carapace of the bug and it toppled.

"Damn." Jason aimed his own rifle and began firing as more bugs began to appear. "I think we found the nest."

Mantis-like bugs were crawling along the walls and ceiling. Others were rising out of the gunk in the holding tank.

Jason fired a pair of shots and watched a bug fall from the ceiling into the holding tank with a splash. "I'd say we definitely found the nest."

The clicking of mandibles was loud. Then several bugs emitted hissing shrieks.

"We found the nest!" Jason yelled into his comm. "Confirmed. I see twelve, maybe twenty bugs." He was only giving a quick count. *Accuracy be damned*!

"*Are you gonna be okay?*" Damian asked. "*We can send you support.*"

"We're way beyond the help of reinforcements." *We'll be dead long before anyone else arrives here.* Jason fired his rifle again. "I think we have the situation under control." He could not believe how easily he spoke the lie.

"*But, Jason, you—*"

"Now we need to seal this place off good and tight." Mark aimed his rifle towards a cylindrical piece of equipment. "Can you damage that pump?"

"Not with these rifles." Jason shook his head. PPGs were designed to have their plasma bursts dissipate on impact, rather than damage equipment or bulkheads.

A bug loomed up in front of the opening, its claws raised to strike.

Mark shot it. "Got any grenades?"

"Yeah, but it's only a S-30 *FlashBang*." Jason pulled it out of his pocket. "It might work." He primed and threw it towards the pump. "Watch your eyes!"

The explosion was loud and bright, but the grenade was designed more to distract opponents than to actually damage things.

Bugs shrieked. Several lost their grip on the walls and ceilings and fell into the tank. Others continued to move around the tank's edge, pawing at their eyes. Obviously blinded, one staggered into a fellow drone and they both hacking at each other with their claws.

A stray slash tore through the pump's casing.

"Yes!" Mark opened fire on the broken metal.

Jason followed suit.

The bugs continued to shriek and several resumed their climb towards the two humans. Mandibles clicked loudly.

Sparks erupted from the pump.

"That's done it!" Mark crowed.

"Done what?"

A ripple spread across the surface of the holding tank.

"We've killed the pump...now the automated systems will kick in."

Hatches began to close, sealing off the tubes and pipes which emptied into the tank.

Jason took a step back as a hatch dropped from the ceiling to seal off the pipe he and Mark were inside.

The *clunk* as it sealed was loud.

· Chapter Eighteen

"The nest is sealed." Jason ignored the looks he was getting as he stepped through the hatch and back into the cramped access room. He felt exhausted after that trek and the firefight. His uniform was filthy, with half-dried splashes marking the fabric well-past his waist.

"You're sure about that?" Damian asked. He and Joshua were facing the hatch, with their rifles in their hands.

Mark climbed out through the hatch. He let his rifle drop onto the floor. "Yech," he grumbled. His blue jeans were a uniform brown in colour now, glistening wetly in the florescent lights with an oily sheen. "That was just as bad as I thought it would be." He hit the keypad and the heavy hatch swung closed. It locked with a solid *thunk*.

Eloyda Acuna looked at them with concern on her face. She was obviously checking them over for obvious injuries.

"You're sure?" Damian repeated.

"We dropped the pressure hatches around the main holding tank. It'll take a blast-pack to get through. Should be strong enough to stop even those *things*. They won't be getting back out."

"Good to hear." Eloyda paused, giving them another look. "You two are a *mess*."

"I know."

"You should go and wash that stuff off yourselves immediately. It can't be good to have any of it on your skin. It's certainly not sterile."

"I never would have guessed that." From the nauseated expressions which the others were wearing, Jason was glad that his sense of smell was still missing in action. He looked down at himself. *Yep, I'm looking forward to a nice long hot shower.* "Damian, monitor the reclamation system for any signs of breaches."

"Will do." The militia officer nodded. "What precisely did you guys do to it?"

"We smashed the pumping system." Mark hooked his thumb at the hatch. "That triggered the pressure doors to seal and also started to fill the main tank with effluent. The bugs are gonna drown."

"If they breath," Eloyda commented.

"Or at least they'll be held securely until we can get a proper military team in here to deal with them." Jason paused. "Any sign of other roaming bugs?"

"Nothing on the cameras. Chuck's been watching carefully. He even got a few more security cameras to start working. He's seen nothing."

"Okay."

Damian was wrinkling his nose. "Corporal, you should go and clean up. We can handle things without you."

Jason eyed him. "You're sure about that?"

"Yeah, really sure."

Joshua was nodding his head. "Yeah, you stink."

Mark tugged on his arm. "Come on, Jason, let's hit the showers."

"What about the rest of the mission? We still need to return to Trove and—"

"It can wait." Eloyda gestured. "Hit the showers."

"You're sure that the nest is sealed?"

"Yes, Damian, it's sealed tight."

Damian nodded. "Then go clean up. We can report in later."

"I'm not sure that the director will—"

"Riley won't have any choice," Eloyda interrupted. "We've temporarily lost contact with Trove."

"What?" Jason took a step towards Ops. "When did—"

"Go and shower!" Damian pleaded. "I'll work on regaining contact with Director Riley. You aren't coming into Ops smelling like that." He managed a weak smile. "I'll ask Franco to shoot you if you do."

Eloyda nodded. "I'll have you both quarantined."

"Come on." Mark tugged gently on his arm. "She's got really big needles she likes to drag out for quarantine patients."

Eloyda gave him a wide and entirely too cheerful smile.

"Let them work."

"All right." Jason nodded his head with some reluctance.

"Oh, one question." Eloyda paused, as if uncertain how to continue. "Did you find any sign of the others?"

"We found one of Fiona's legs." Jason darted a quick glance towards Mark.

The other man had twitched, but he didn't look ready to break down.

"No sign of Brad at all."

"Damn."

Jason followed Mark into the tiny bathroom. "This place is tiny." They had already shucked off their breastplates and helmets and left their rifles in the main office. The office held a desk and two chairs—and was barely large enough for that much furniture.

"It was only meant for the Ops staff to use during emergency situations." Without warning, Mark pulled Jason in close and gave him a kiss. "I'd call it *intimate*."

"This is hardly the best time for this."

"I know...but I want it anyway." Mark pressed himself more tightly against Jason. "And so do you."

Jason felt himself growing hard inside his coveralls. Their faces were close enough that he could feel Mark's warm breath and their cheeks grazed. Feeling the other man's stubble against his own struck Jason as the hottest sensation ever.

"You do want it." Mark reached down and grabbed Jason through his coveralls.

Jason grunted. "Yeah." He couldn't deny it.

Mark turned on the shower and warm water immediately soaked them both.

Jason scrubbed his hands through his hair. "That feels so good," he murmured.

Mark smiled at him, before bending down to pull off his boots. "And now we can have some fun." He started peeling off his soaked tee-shirt.

Jason grabbed him and gave him another kiss. His tongue probed deeply into Mark's mouth. "You are one hot piece of ass," he said. "I've wanted you from the first moment I saw you."

"I think you're pretty hot yourself," Mark replied. "The blow-job in the office was just a tease."

"Yeah, it was."

Mark let his hands drop down to unzip his jeans.

Jason quickly followed suit, unzipping his coveralls. He managed to step out of them, letting his uniform drop the floor of the shower. The warm spray was sluicing away grime and gunk, and the tenting of their soaked boxer shorts left nothing to either of their imaginations.

Mark instinctively reached for Jason's cock through his boxers and they kissed passionately.

Jason broke the embrace and adjusted the shower temperature. He turned back around and they kissed again, their hands exploring each other's bodies and their tongues probing deeply into each other's mouths.

Mark peeled off his boxers and let his erect cock spring forward.

"Very nice," Jason murmured. His own boxers were straining to contain his own throbbing hard-on. "I want to suck that beauty."

They stood under the warm jet of the shower and kissed some more. Their cocks rubbed against each other and Jason ran his hands down Mark's furry chest. He couldn't resist any longer and dropped down onto his knees.

Mark moaned softly as Jason devoured his cock.

Jason was making his own grunting sounds as he took each of Mark's balls into his mouth, abandoning them just long enough to suck the tip of his lover's cock while Mark moaned with ecstasy. Jason licked his way up and down Mark's long thick shaft, played with his balls, and then reached his hand around to start playing with his tight hole.

Mark moaned even louder. "Fuck me," he gasped.

"Are you sure?"

"Hell yes! I've wanted this since I sucked you off." Mark pulled Jason to his feet to kiss him again. "When I thought we were going to die, I wanted my last thoughts to be about you. So fuck me!"

Jason grinned. "If you're sure."

Mark squirted liquid soap into his hands and quickly lathered up Jason's cock.

Jason eyed his partner's ass, and started slowly working his fingers in. The further he slid his fingers inside, the louder Mark moaned—which got Jason even more turned on.

"Fuck me," Mark pleaded.

"You got it." Jason lathered more soap onto his rock-hard cock and positioned the head. His cock slid in fairly easily and both men moaned with delight. Jason teased him, and then began to slide more of his shaft in.

Mark winced, but protested when Jason tried to pull back out. "No, keep going! Just take it slow." He arched his back a bit more. "Damn that feels good."

"How long has it been for you?"

"Too long." Mark grunted. "No one on Titan worth bothering with."

"No?" Jason worked his cock all the way in, until his balls rested on the other man's muscular cheeks. "There are a few cuties around here."

"But total wastes in personality."

Jason smiled. *I heard similar things about you,* he thought. He pulled his cock halfway out of Mark's ass, and then slid back in again, repeating this motion over and getting faster and harder. He was pulling out far enough that just his head was still remaining inside Mark's hole, before burying his shaft so deep inside him again that his balls slapped against Mark's ass.

The shower beat down on them.

Mark grunted as Jason fucked him harder and harder. "Yeah, keep doing that!" he begged. "It's been so long."

Jason kept thrusting. He was getting close to the edge.

Mark was panting heavily. He had wrapped one of his hands around his own cock and was stroking himself furiously.

"Oh my God!" Jason gave one final thrust and felt himself cum.

"Gah!" Mark's felt his ass tighten, and then he staggered as he shot his own load all over the shower tiles.

Jason was still feeling weak in the knees. "Good thing's there's no shortage of hot water around here."

Mark chuckled as he finally turned the shower off. "Yeah, I know." They'd soaped each other up again and washed away the traces of their love-making. "You were amazing."

"Thanks."

"It's been too long since I've had a decent session with anyone." Mark reached for a towel hanging on the wall. "Too bad we aren't back in Trove...my quarters are nice and close to the showers there."

Jason sighed with regret. "That would have been nice." He picked up his soaked uniform. "At least it smells better now." He eyed Mark's clothing—the jeans were still badly stained.

"Hang on." Mark had quickly wrapped the towel around his waist and gone into the main office.

"Where are you going?" Jason followed him. He was glad that no one else was around. *I'm the ranking officer for the Pouncers now...I won't have much authority if they see me prancing around naked.*

"Ha! I thought so." Mark turned around from the desk. He tossed a bundle of clothing towards Jason. "You can wear that for now."

"What is it?" Jason shook it out.

"A basic coverall." Mark was already pulling on an identical drab green outfit. "Nothing fancy, but it's something. Certainly not armour. Not even an anti-ballistic weave."

"It will do though." Jason finished zipping it up. The material felt rough against his skin, though he was willing to admit that his cock was still overly sensitive as an after effect from the sexual romp. "It will do though." He pulled his boots out of the shower.

* * *

"You going native on us?" Franco asked as Jason and Mark stepped into the operations centre. "You defecting?"

"Hardly." Other than their own boots, both men were wearing the drab green jump-suits. Jason set his rifle on top of a console. Mark had cleaned off their body armour and Jason had given the PPG rifles a quick cleaning after their shower. *I'm taking no chances that this thing will jam if we're attacked by more bugs,* he thought.

Eloyda was chewing on a ration bar. She eyed them and nodded her head in approval.

Joshua was pale-faced, but sitting at a computer and typing in commands while he watched monitors.

Chuck and Tyler were seated at other terminals.

"What do you see, Josh?"

"Not too much right now. The hallways are deserted."

"Everything is shutting down," Damian complained. There was no mistaking the irritation in his voice. "I think the director did something via remote."

"Oh?"

"The systems started going out an hour or so ago. Just before you two came back."

"Could it be part of the damage we caused?"

Mark shook his head. "That shouldn't have effected any other systems." He moved across Ops to the computer where Damian was sitting. "Chuck, did you take a look at this?"

"Yeah, but I can't figure it out. The power system is not responding to any of my codes. It's like the Cradle is hibernating."

"It just might be doing that." Jason frowned. "Or it could be a remote."

"Life support is still working. We have heat and light." Damian gestured. "We still have access to the security cameras too."

"Still, it's a good thing that we're making plans to leave. What is the status of the reclamation tank?"

"The locks around life support are all holding. The system itself is issuing an increasing number of complaints about pressure building up."

"From what?"

"The sewage and water lines are sealed. There's no place for any of it to go now. The holding tanks are only so big."

Jason winced.

Mark looked at him rather guiltily.

Jason shook his head without saying a word. *And we just took* how long *of a shower? Damn it!* The universe hated him. "How long will before it becomes critical?"

"Depends on how much you want to shower and drink. A few days maybe."

"And then what?"

"Then the regular pipes back-up and we hope none of them burst. Eventually the clean tanks will run dry too."

"Great. Any word from Director Riley?"

"No contact." Damian shook his head. "From what Tyler can tell, the comm-system is working but Trove isn't talking back to us."

"They can hear us, but they're not saying anything?"

"Not a word."

"Wonderful." Jason wondered if this had all been part of the company's plan for them. *Send us in to get killed by the bugs so the real security teams can learn how to deal with them safely.*

"We can't stay here much longer," Eloyda argued from her chair. "We should go back to Trove now."

"I know, but we can't risk the bugs getting loose. I'm not sure that they'll actually drown...or even that we trapped them all."

Franco snorted. "So, what's the plan, Corp?"

"This facility is compromised. Seriously." Jason checked the ammo-clip in his pistol. *Full charge.* "We need to blow the reactor."

"Blow the reactor?" Damian stared at him.

Franco threw his head back and roared with laughter. "I knew I liked you."

"Isn't that a bit extreme?" Eloyda asked. "I mean, this facility is—"

"Thoroughly infested, Doctor. We need to...what would be the right clinical term? Cauterize the wound?"

"You believe that we are beyond quarantine then?"

"Completely."

She frowned at him.

Mark nodded his agreement. "He's right."

"I thought the labs were impregnable."

"This a biological research facility, Damian." Tyler coughed into his hand. "It's designed to be capable of total immolation...just in case something nasty gets loose."

"I got news for you...something nasty *is* loose." Jason turned to Mark. "Well? What do we have to do?"

Mark called up a display onto the computer. "The fusion plant is down on level four. If it explodes, it'll take out this entire facility."

"Pretty good failsafe."

"Company policy. Leave nothing for any rivals to use."

"Can you blow it from here?"

"Yes, I think so."

"What about Trove?" Jason looked at the two techs. "What happens to Trove if we blow the Cradle?"

"It's far enough way that it won't be destroyed by the blast. Not if the tunnel bulkheads are sealed."

Tyler nodded his agreement. "It's on a separate failsafe."

"Good enough for me." Jason gestured to everyone. "Pack up your gear. Mark, use the computer to start rigging the reactor. Give us enough time to reach the garage and get back to Trove before it all blows."

"You got it." He moved to the computer terminal.

Eloyda was shaking her head.

"Do you have something to say, Doctor?"

"I'm just a civilian," she replied after a moment. "This is a security matter. It's in your hands."

Jason gave her a smile. "It's gonna be a spectacular end to my career," he told her.

· Chapter Nineteen

The dust-buggy pulled into the garage and its hatches popped open.

"Where have you been?" Claire Riley stared at the exhausted looking faces of the remaining members of the security team as they appeared from inside the vehicle. She had a cluster of men standing behind her.

"Touring the Cradle." Jason wasn't carrying his rifle, but he did rest his hand on his holstered pistol. "Fighting a rather nasty bug infestation." His drab green overalls hung loosely on him—the size was wrong.

Franco dropped to the ground, cradling his heavy rifle. He gave the director an unpleasant smile.

Damian watched as the garage airlock closed with a solid *thunk*.

Eloyda was directing Tyler and Chuck as they helped Joshua dismount from the buggy. She did not even look towards Claire.

Mark moved to stand beside Jason, wearing borrowed body armour over his coveralls, and holding a rifle. He didn't *quite* aim it towards Claire.

She glared at all of them. "You've been out of contact for days. I was preparing to send a second team." She waved towards the eight men standing behind her.

Jason eyed them. They were all wearing *WY-2/BX Hostile Environment Armour*. He was impressed by their preparation. The cloth inner layer could maintain temperature and breathable air for twelve hours, while the outer layer was composed of fifteen armoured plates, all tough enough to withstand a PPG burst. "You've got connections," he said. "Those are top-line suits." *Usually limited to militia or the Guards.*

"We manufacture them." Claire smiled back at him. Her expression was one of false sweetness.

Jason nodded. "Good to know." The men were holding *Mauser CG-PR* rifles as well. *More non-civilian gear. She is not playing games now.* Of course, he had another question raised by their appearance. *Where the hell did they come from?* He had never seen any of these men before.

Eloyda took note of the extra guards. Her eyes narrowed.

"Where is the rest of your team?" Claire asked. "I've been trying to raise Sergeant Foster for several hours."

Liar, Jason thought. "He's dead. So is Terry Sisler. And Brad Kellar. And Fiona Steele. And pretty much everyone else assigned to the Cradle except for Tyler and Chuck there." Jason hooked his thumb back at the two techs.

They started nervously. Neither man looked happy to be there at the moment. They were eying the director and the eight guards with equal trepidation.

Claire glanced towards the techs, her eyes narrowing slightly. Then she looked at Jason again. "All of them are dead? You have confirmed that?"

"We didn't find their bodies, Director, but we searched the whole complex. We should have found some trace of them. If they were alive."

Claire slowly nodded her head. "I see. And how did you manage to survive then?"

"Battlefield luck."

"I see."

The ground shuddered violently, making everyone stumble and stagger. Small chunks of rock broke loose from the ceiling and crashed onto the floor.

Joshua bounced against the buggy.

One of Claire's guards cried out as a rock bounced off his arm. "Damn it!"

Eloyda dropped to one knee.

The tremor subsided.

"What the hell was that?" one of Claire's guards cried out.

"Just a Titanquake," Claire snapped at them. "Stop panicking!" She did not seem afraid, merely angry.

"No, it was more than that." Jason rode out the tremors with just a slight flexing of his legs. "That, Director, was the detonation of a nuclear reactor."

Her jaw dropped open. "You don't mean—"

"The Cradle is no longer in operation."

"You idiot!" she snarled. "Do you have any idea of what you've just done?" She took a step towards him and her guards raised their rifles.

Jason's companions raised their own.

Eloyda gasped.

Claire froze in mid-step, and then licked her lips.

Jason stared back at her.

Claire took a deep breath. "Do you have any idea at all?" she demanded of Jason. She still didn't move though. She glared at Mark as well.

Jason made no response to her.

"You, *Corporal*, have destroyed a vital and extremely expensive research facility. Millions of credits of equipment and resources. The loss of knowledge and data alone—"

"I know exactly what I've done, *Director*." Jason's voice was quiet. "I eradicated a nest of extremely dangerous bugs."

"Those *bugs* were all part of a controlled experiment. You have no idea of what mysteries they could have answered!"

Eloyda snorted. "Director, that *controlled experiment* cost the lives of over a dozen of my colleagues."

"*Accidents* happen, Doctor."

"Those bugs are deadly," Jason pointed out.

"Anything can be deadly," Claire told him calmly. "If not monitored and used properly. We have safeguards in place. They were part of an experiment."

Franco snorted at that.

Mark shook his head. He kept his borrowed rifle aimed towards Claire.

"They were a miracle of evolution here on Titan. We could have learned so much from them."

"If they were natives."

"What was that, Tyler?"

The tech brushed his lank hair out of his eyes. He blinked and swallowed nervously as she stared at him. "I overhead some of the tech-heads talking. They were saying that the subjects—I guess they meant those bugs—didn't come from Titan. They were pretty sure they had evolved somewhere else."

"An unproven theory." Claire shook her head. "And unless we can find another nest to study, it will remain unproven...thanks to Mister Shaw."

"Corporal Shaw."

"I do not recognize your rank," Claire replied coldly. "I should have you up on charges. Breach of contract. Vandalism of company property. Destruction of company property. Yu-Wei has very fine lawyers on permanent retainer."

"Yes, and what will the courts think about the company's research?" Damian demanded. "Last time I checked, the Colonial Guard took a very harsh view of biological engineering."

For a moment, there was silence in the garage.

Then Claire laughed. "The Guard have their own little bio-weapons division," she told him contemptuously. "They subcontract out a fair amount of research and development projects to various companies and corporations. Things they'd rather not have to deal with themselves. You'd be surprised at what those contracts can be worth."

"So now what?" Jason asked her. He was eying her loyal guards-the men held their weapons like well-trained professionals, not amateurs.

He could sense Mark standing close to his shoulder. "Do we just continue this little standoff until someone loses it and starts shooting?"

Claire grimaced.

Franco adjusted his grip on his rifle. He seemed perfectly at ease.

"I suggest that we take a break." Eloyda Acuna stepped between the two groups. She moved slowly and carefully though. "I know that we're all tired and somewhat on edge. Mistakes will happen."

Claire frowned at her.

So did Jason.

"Director, you've been under a lot of pressure as well. Given the communication blackout, you must have been preparing for a worst case scenario. Invasion and the like. We should all take a breather and get some rest before continuing this discussion."

Jason's jaw was hanging open.

"Doctor, I think you might have a good idea there." Claire managed to sound impressed and happy with the suggestion. "Yes, I do think that taking a break would be a very good idea for us all." She turned her head. "Stand down."

Jason nodded, suspicious even though the other guards were lowering their rifles. *Half-trained researchers or real security professionals? Where did you get these men, Director?* "I agree." He waved at his squad-mates to lower their own weapons.

Mark was the last to do so.

"You should retire to your quarters and rest." Claire managed to sound civil. "We can meet in a few hours to talk about the status of your contract with Yu-Wei."

"Thank you, Director." Jason nodded to her. "We'll do that."

"An excellent decision, Director." Acuna gave them all a warm smile as she walked closer to the Pouncers. "Mark, get them out of here."

He stared at her. "What?"

"Take one of the shuttles and get your friends off Titan. They'll be a lot safer out in space." She looked over her shoulder, but Claire was talking to Tyler and Chuck.

Neither technician looked happy, but they were both listening to her and nodding occasionally.

Her guards were watching the Pouncers though.

"You have to get off Titan," Eloyda pressed in a soft tone of voice. "Quickly."

"Claire has never taken defeat very well," Mark agreed.

"She could arrange for an accident," Eloyda continued. "If you all died, there'd be no one to contradict whatever story she wants to tell the company. She's going to need to spin something to cover up the Cradle disaster. Having your bodies on hand as saboteurs would be rather useful."

"What about you?"

"I'm Trove's chief doctor. She won't hurt me. I certainly wasn't in charge of anything that happened in the Cradle. I had to agree with whatever the 'heavily-armed maniac soldiers' ordered me to do." She laughed quietly. "I have protection enough of my own—I cured the daughter of one of Yu-Wei's vice presidents. Rather embarrassing little souvenir of a trip off-world and a rather odd romantic encounter. He was very happy that I am discrete." She glanced back towards the director again. "Get going...I can't cover your absence for very long, but I'll do what I can."

"Thanks," Jason told her.

Eloyda smiled at him. "Go to your quarters and get some rest," she said in a loud voice. "Doctor's orders. I'll be along in a bit to check on you all. I'll bring some sedatives to help you sleep if you need it."

"Thank you, Doctor." Jason made sure that his voice carried to where Claire was still lecturing the two technicians. "I know that resting in our bunks is just what we need right now."

"Thanks for everything, Eloyda." Mark gave her a smile and then turned to Jason. "Come on then."

Jason signalled the others to follow.

"In our bunks?" Franco asked.

"Yeah, we're going to our quarters."

"We have an armed stand-off with those punks and now we're just gonna go quietly to bed?"

"Trust me, Franco." Jason patted his arm. "Keep your voice down. Smile. And follow my orders."

"Fine."

Damian was eying him. "You heard the corporal, Franco."

Franco was now helping support Joshua as they moved away from the buggy. Franco was grumbling under his breath.

"I'm fine," the security guard argued. "She gave me a shot of something. I'm feeling no pain. None at all."

Damian chuckled. "Yep, he's flying high."

"We can't wait for you to stand up if you fall down," Franco told him. "Anyway, I'm gonna use you as a shield in case anyone does start shooting."

Jason managed not to laugh aloud at that. *Some things never change,* he thought. *The squad goes on, even with our losses.*

The door to the garage closed behind them and the squad relaxed slightly.

Mark hurriedly led though the corridor.

Damian slowed his steps to fall in beside Jason. "I've got copies of the full mission records," he said, giving the other man a nod.

"Of what?"

"Of our mission to the Cradle of course. We can blow up any story Claire tries to tell about us."

"How'd you get that?"

"I can hack anything, remember?"

"Thanks." Jason glanced over his shoulder. No one was following them.

Their feet made very little noise on the floor.

Mark paused outside one room. "Hang on." He hit the keypad and it slid open. There was no one inside. He hurried to a small computer terminal and hastily typed in a code. He paused while the small monitor flickered and flashed, then he continued typing in commands. "I'm putting in an order to prep a shuttle for us."

"Won't that alert Claire?"

"No, I'm using Fiona's access codes. Not mine. The computer will automatically route the work order without anyone in admin being informed. I hope," he muttered softly.

Jason frowned.

"Now, let's get to your quarters." Mark led them back into the corridor. "Come on."

"Why bother with our quarters?" Damian asked.

"Yeah," Franco grunted. "Why not just run for the shuttle now?"

"We need to stop by your quarters first. Claire might be monitoring them, waiting for you to arrive there—watching for the doors to open, lights to come on, et cetera. She won't want to take chances on us running freely through Trove and raising hell."

"Good thinking."

Jason nodded. *I haven't seen anyone around here either. Where's the rest of Trove's staff? Did Claire send them on errands to keep away any witnesses?*

"Anyway," Mark continued, "I thought that you might want to gather up any personal effects of yours. I don't think Yu-Wei will be willing to ship your gear back to home base after this."

"Not bloody likely." Damian shook his head.

Jason looked up as the door to his quarters hissed open. He felt his heart-rate speed up. *Is this it?*

Mark stepped through, a casual grin on his face. He had strapped a Colonial Guard-issue backpack over his shoulders. "You ready to go, Jason?"

"Past ready." Jason had changed out of his borrowed drab green jumpsuit for a pair of blue jeans and a loose tee-shirt. "We're going for the casual look, right?" His own pack was stuffed with clothing and a handful of possessions he didn't want to leave behind.

"Yep." Mark nodded. His own black jeans and tight red tee-shirt clung to his body in all the right ways. "We're ready to move."

Jason leaned in and kissed Mark on the lips.

Mark kissed him back.

"Can't you two do that later?" Eloyda demanded from the open doorway.

With reluctance, Jason pulled himself away from Mark. "Spoilsport."

"Plenty of time once we're off Titan." Mark gestured. "Let's go."

Jason stepped into the corridor and watched the door to his quarters hiss closed. He kept looking around while Eloyda moved to the next door and entered a code into its locked keypad. "How much time do you think we have?"

"Not that much."

"I should be able to win you a few hours at least." Eloyda gave him a smile. "The security logs will show that I came to your quarters and gave you a sedative to help all of you rest."

Franco stepped into the hallway. "Let me tell you that I think this sucks." His muscles bulged through his civilian clothing. "I feel naked without my rifle."

"We want to try to get away from Titan without starting a firefight," Jason snapped at him. "We're in disguise." The squad would be less noticeable in their civilian clothes than hurrying through the corridors in their BCM uniforms. *Or so we hope.* To his mind, the squad still looked like a group of soldiers.

Eloyda opened the last door and Joshua hobbled out. "Good-bye, Mark. Good luck."

"Thank you, Doctor." Mark gave her a hug. "Thanks for everything you've done for us."

"Your shuttle should be prepped by now. I'll buy you as much time as I can down here." Eloyda gave him another smile. "If you launch in about twelve minutes, you should be able to leave without being spotted by anyone."

Jason frowned. "The tracking room—"

"Will be unmanned. Nathan is on duty and I fear that he's going to sleep through most of his shift. That last cup of coffee he had was not as strong as he might have hoped. A good night's sleep will do him good."

Mark was grinning. "Thank you again."

"Just get going...and don't get caught."

"We won't." Mark watched the doctor hurry down the corridor. "Come on...we don't have a lot of time."

"Nope, we don't." Jason shook his head. "Straight to the launch pad."

Mark hurried towards the elevator, with the squad following after him.

No one around, Jason noted. *This works to our advantage.*

Mark glanced at him and gave him a smile.

Jason smiled back. "Remind me to show you the Martian Shipyards when we get back to civilization. That should put you in right mood."

"I'm looking forward to it, Jason."

Also by Frank Sol

Novels Of The Sensual City
A Family Affair
Delivering The Goods
Divine Punishment
Good Neighbours
Just Between Friends
Landscaping, Manscaping
Titan's Cradle - A Novel of the Sensual Suns

Novels On The Prairies
Bareback Range
Return To Bareback Range
Fenced In